DELIVER US FROM EVIL

A. ROUCHER

Roucher

I would like to thank my wife, for always allowing me to chase my crazy ideas and for her help proof reading this book.

Table of Contents

Roucher

Chapter 1

Patrick Sullivan – Ranger, Mosul

"In campis sanguinis ambulat; militem sequitur sicut frater."
He walks in fields of blood; he follows the soldier like a
brother.

The night smelled of dust and cordite, a dry heat clinging even after sundown. Mosul's Old City was a labyrinth of crumbling walls, alleys narrower than a man's shoulders, windows bricked with cinderblock or covered by sheets of rusted tin. Specialist Patrick Sullivan, Ranger Battalion, shifted the weight of his kit as he followed his squad down a broken street. Boots crunched over shattered tile and brass casings.

They had been moving since dusk, clearing buildings one at a time. The insurgents had fled weeks ago, but the city still groaned with pockets of resistance snipers, hidden IEDs, men with nothing left but a rifle and the promise of paradise. Patrick's shoulders ached. Sweat darkened the strap of his rifle.

"Eyes up, Sergeant Kearney whispered from the front. His voice rasped in Patrick's headset. We're coming up on the church."

Patrick's pulse quickened. He had read about Mosul, Iraq in high school, seen pictures of the ancient churches, their spires rising above the skyline before the war. Now, as the patrol turned into a narrow square, he saw what was left of one.

The Syriac Orthodox Mar Thomas Church loomed like a wounded giant. The facade was peppered with bullet holes. One tower had collapsed entirely, leaving a jagged pile of stone and rebar. The door hung off its hinges. Icons of Christ and the Virgin had been defaced, their eyes gouged out with knives. Charred wood stained the stone black.

"Clear it," Kearney ordered.

Two men stacked on the doorway, weapons up. Patrick took rear security, scanning the rooftops. His breath echoed in his ears. Somewhere a dog barked. A generator rattled far off. Then silence. The team moved inside.

The nave stretched wide and skeletal. Benches lay overturned. Moonlight filtered through holes in the roof, falling in shafts thick with dust. The altar was cracked down the center like split bone. The smell of burned incense clung stubbornly to the air, fighting with mold and smoke. Patrick swept his muzzle across the shadows. His beam caught on fragments of stained-glass glittering-like blood on the floor. A shape startled him, Mary's face, broken into pieces, her gaze scattered.

"Clear," Corporal Diaz muttered.

Patrick moved toward the sacristy, careful of his steps. The others spread out, checking rooms and stairwells. The silence pressed heavy, as though the air itself waited. Then he saw it. Beneath a collapsed shelf, half-buried in stone dust, a box glinted. Gold leaf cracked with age. Its lid split open from some explosion, hinges torn. The remains of a reliquary. Patrick's throat tightened. His mother had once shown him relics in Boston, little fragments of saints' bones, glass vials of dust. He remembered being a boy, staring at them in wonder.

"Hey," Diaz called. "Find something?"

Patrick knelt, brushing debris aside. Inside the broken box, a small bundle of silk remained intact, folded tight. Even through grime, the embroidery shone, red threads forming Syriac script. He couldn't read it, but the characters looked old, impossibly old. He reached in, fingertips brushing the fabric.

Heat surged through his hand. Not the warmth of cloth but the sear of iron on fire. His breath caught. For a moment he wasn't in Mosul. The desert stretched endless under a sky the color of bleached bone. Wind hissed across dunes; in the center, bound by chains that writhed like serpents, was a figure, neither man nor beast, its form shifting, cloaked in light so bright it burned and shadow so deep it swallowed the sand. The figure turned, there was no face, only hollowness where light collapsed inward. Patrick staggered back, heart pounding. His squad leader's voice crackled in his ear:

"Sullivan, what the hell are you doing? Move!"

The vision snapped away. The relic was only a bone sliver wrapped in cloth, cool and fragile in his hand. He tucked it quickly into his pocket, too shaken to explain. They finished the sweep and moved out.

The days after, Patrick couldn't shake the feeling of being followed. At night, in the half-sleep between watch rotations, he heard whispers. Not Arabic. Not English. Words curling at the edge of comprehension, like someone speaking under water. He woke sweating, palm aching where he had touched the relic.

"Man, you look like shit," Diaz said one morning, passing him a canteen.

"You dreaming or something?"

Patrick forced a laugh. "Yeah. Something like that."

He didn't tell them what he saw. How could he? Soldiers teased enough for less, but the visions grew. On patrol, he caught glimpses of a man in doorways, staring with blank hollows where eyes should be. In the market, among burned-out stalls, he swore he heard chains dragging. Once, on guard duty, he blinked and found the desert before him again, the chained figure straining, its whisper curling into his ear:

"Fides fracta aperit januam."
Broken faith opens the door.

He jolted awake, rifle slipping from his grasp. Two weeks later, his squad launched a raid on a suspected insurgent hideout in a dense block of concrete apartments. Night vision goggles cast everything green, phosphorescent. They stacked on the door, breacher in place.

"Three, two, one"

The door blew inward. Rangers stormed in. Gunfire erupted, sudden and deafening. Bullets smacked into plaster. Patrick moved with the squad, clearing room to room. His heartbeat thundered. Then he saw him. A man stood at the hallway's end, robes fluttering though the air was still. His face was veiled in light and shadow, chains rattling at his feet. Patrick froze.

"Contact front!" he shouted, firing.

His rounds sparked against concrete, nothing there. The squad leader swore.

"Sullivan! Nothing there! Move!"

But Patrick saw him, clear as daylight, moving closer. He kept firing. His rounds punched holes in the wall. Then, an RPG slammed the building. The blast threw Patrick backward. Heat engulfed him, ears ringing, lungs screaming. He landed on his back, vision spinning. The last thing he saw was the figure looming over him, chains unwinding, voice whispering like a lover:

"Brother."

Then darkness. When they found him, Patrick's body was still warm, his rifle clutched tight. His palm bore a faint burn scar, as though he had pressed it against fire.

Homecoming & Relic's Return

The cardboard shipping crate sat on the Sullivan family's dining room table, sealed with military tape and scrawled with a return address from Kuwait. Its presence filled the house with a silence thicker than grief. Nora Sullivan stood with trembling hands on the box, her rosary dangling from her wrist. Sean sat opposite her, arms folded, jaw tight. Ashlyn hovered at the edge of the kitchen doorway, unable to step closer.

It had been three weeks since the Army chaplain's knock at the door. Three weeks since Nora collapsed on the porch steps, keening like her own mother had once done at wakes in Galway. Three weeks since Sean poured Jameson into a chipped glass and smashed the bottle against the sink, unwilling to let the liquor outlive his son. Now all that remained of Patrick was inside this box.

"Do you want me to?" Sean began, his voice low and gravelly.

"No," Nora cut him off.

She fumbled for the scissors and slit the tape. The cardboard flaps gave way with a groan. Inside, wrapped in brown paper and careful inventory tags, lay Patrick's belongings. His boots, scuffed and caked with desert dust. His uniform blouse, torn at the sleeve. Dog tags, metal cold even in the warmth of the kitchen. A pocket Bible, leather cover cracked. A photograph of the three of them on the Cape, Patrick's arm around Ashlyn, all of them sunburnt and smiling.

Nora lifted each piece as though it were relics of a saint. Her lips moved in silent prayer. When she reached the Bible, she paused. The leather was warped, as though singed at the edges. She opened it, and something slid free, a folded square of ancient silk. The threads were frayed, the red embroidery dulled with age, but the words still glimmered faintly: Syriac script, unfamiliar and beautiful. Inside the silk was a sliver of bone, ivory-yellow, no larger than her thumbnail.

"What's that?" Sean asked, frowning.

"Something from his pack," Nora whispered.

"Maybe… maybe a gift. Maybe he wanted it blessed."

Ashlyn leaned in, curiosity battling fear. The bone fragment caught the light strangely, throwing a faint glimmer as though wet. She reached out before she could think better of it.

The moment her fingertips brushed the silk, warmth bled into her skin. Not the comforting warmth of a blanket or a hearth, but something sharp, insistent, like the heat of a coal just before it burns. She flinched, pulling back, but not before an image flickered in her mind: sand stretching endless, chains rattling across the dunes, a hollow voice whispering her name. She gasped.

"Lyn?"

Sean's head snapped up.

"Nothing, she said quickly, pressing her hand to her chest. Her heart hammered. Just a shock. Static."

Her parents didn't notice the faint red mark on her palm, shaped like a circle. Nora wrapped the silk and bone carefully and set it back inside the Bible, tucking it against her breast as if it were treasure.

"It came home with him, she murmured. Then it's ours to keep."

That night, Ashlyn couldn't sleep. She sat cross-legged on her bed, Patrick's Bible open before her. The silk-wrapped fragment seemed to pulse faintly in the lamplight, the embroidered script shifting like ripples on water. She thought of Patrick, his laugh, his steady hand on her shoulder when she was scared, the way he called her "Lyn" instead of her full name. Her throat tightened.

"I miss you," she whispered.

The relic gave no answer, only a quiet heat that traveled up her arm, curling behind her ear like a breath.

For a moment she thought she heard his voice, distant, muffled, as if through a wall:

"Lyn ..."

She shut the Bible fast and shoved it beneath her pillow, pressing both hands over her ears. Downstairs, Sean sat in the dark with a glass of water, staring at the flag folded tight on the mantle. Nora knelt in front of the family crucifix, praying through tears. The house groaned with the weight of their absence and their grief, and in the silence of her room, Ashlyn dreamed of chains clinking in the sand.

The Wake

The funeral home smelled of lilies and floor polish, that mingling of beauty and antiseptic sorrow. A line of mourners stretched out the door and down the brick steps, each person carrying grief in different ways, old neighbors from Dorchester, classmates from Boston College High, veterans in pressed suits with medals on their chests. The American flag draped over Patrick's coffin shone beneath the overhead lights, its stars sharp, its folds exact.

Ashlyn lingered near the front row with her mother; Patrick's pocket Bible clutched against her ribs. Inside, wrapped in the yellowing silk, the sliver of bone rested like a heartbeat. She hadn't let it out of her sight since it came. Sean stood ramrod straight by the casket, shaking hands until his knuckles went white. His voice stayed even, but his eyes were red rimmed, and when he thought no one was watching, his fingers tapped against the casket lid in restless rhythm, like he expected Patrick to knock back. Nora's rosary clicked endlessly in her hands. She whispered Hail Marys so quickly her lips blurred. Grief radiated from her like a heat, suffocating the air around her.

The soldiers who had come to honor Patrick stood in a tight cluster, their boots polished, their eyes distant. They looked older than their years, shadows under their eyes deeper than exhaustion could explain. One of them crossed himself when he passed the coffin; another muttered something in Spanish and kissed the back of his hand.

At the far end of the room, Father Michael Donnelly adjusted his collar. He had buried too many young men lately, but this one was different. Patrick's death weighed heavy on him, not only because the boy was Irish-Catholic like himself, not only because his mother had begged for the full wake with rosary, priest, and Mass, but because Father Michael could not shake the feeling that there was something off in the air, as though sorrow itself had a second presence.

When he approached the coffin, his eyes caught on the crucifix mounted above it. For a moment, he blinked, unsure. The light from the overhead fixtures threw a shadow on the wall behind, but it wasn't one cross. It was two. The main shadow stood tall and clear, but beside it stretched a darker, sharper twin, warped, like something mimicking the shape without quite belonging.

Father Michael's throat went dry. He closed his eyes, muttered a prayer, and when he opened them again, only one shadow remained. He told himself it was fatigue. As the rosary began, Ashlyn gripped Patrick's Bible tighter. The heat pulsed through the silk-wrapped relic, a warmth that spread through her arm. At first, she thought it was comfort, as if Patrick's presence lingered in the little book, but then, as Father Michael led the mourners in prayer, she heard something slip beneath the words. The Hail Marys echoed around the room, dozens of voices rising and falling, and yet under them all, just faintly, she heard another voice. Familiar. Male. Whispering in her ear.

"Lyn …"

She jolted, eyes darting toward the coffin. Her mother's hand brushed her shoulder, mistaking the shiver for grief.

"It's all right, love. It's all right."

But it wasn't. She could feel the Bible pulsing in her hands like a living thing. Later, after the line of mourners had passed, after the last prayers faded and the crowd thinned, Father Michael lingered near the casket. Sean approached him, jaw tight.

"Father, you'll do the Mass tomorrow?"

"Yes," Father Michael said softly. "At the Cathedral, Patrick deserves the best we can give him."

Sean nodded, gripping Father Michael's hand hard enough to hurt.

"He was a good boy. A soldier. I don't understand why the Lord took him."

Father Michael didn't answer. He had no words that would make sense to a father who had just buried his son. Instead, he squeezed Sean's hand back and offered the only thing he could: presence. As Sean stepped away, Father Michael turned once more to the crucifix. He kept his gaze on it until his eyes burned, daring it to shift, to split again. Nothing. Only the single cross, shadowed on the pale wall. Yet, deep inside, unease settled like ash in his lungs.

That night, in her room, Ashlyn opened the Bible again. She wanted to see the photograph of her brother tucked between the pages, wanted to hold something that still smelled faintly of his sweat and the desert dust, but when she unfolded the silk by candlelight, the script shimmered faintly, as though wet. She traced a letter with her fingertip. Heat surged through her palm, and again, that voice:

"Lyn ..."

Tears blurred her eyes. She pressed the relic to her chest and whispered into the silence,

"I miss you."

Something in the darkness shifted, chains clinking just beyond her hearing.

The Mass at Cathedral of the Holy Cross

The Cathedral of the Holy Cross had not felt so full in years. The towering nave swallowed the crowd in shadows and light, its Gothic arches stretching upward like the ribs of a giant. Flags hung solemnly from the walls; stained glass windows cast fractured colors across marble floors. The great bronze doors had opened that morning to let in a stream of soldiers in dress uniform, family, neighbors, and strangers who had come to honor a young man brought home in a flag-draped coffin.

The casket rested at the head of the aisle, flanked by two soldiers standing rigid at attention. The Stars and Stripes gleamed beneath the cathedral's high vaults, a stark contrast to the dark wooden pews and the muted black of mourning clothes.

Ashlyn sat in the front pew between her parents. Nora's rosary wound so tightly around her fingers the beads dug into her skin. Sean's jaw worked wordlessly, the grief in his face turned to stone. On Ashlyn's lap lay Patrick's Bible, heavy, the relic within pressing against

her thigh like a secret heartbeat. The organ began its
low, thunderous swell. The choir rose, their voices lifting
in solemn chant: In Paradisum deducant te angeli… May
the angels lead you into paradise.

Father Michael Donnelly walked slowly behind the
censer, its chain swinging, smoke rising in pale curls. His
vestments gleamed white and gold, but his face carried
the weight of too many funerals. He sprinkled holy
water across the casket, each droplet catching light
before vanishing against the flag.

"In the name of the Father, and of the Son, and of
the Holy Spirit."

The congregation crossed themselves, murmuring
amen. The Mass unfolded with solemn precision.
Readings from Scripture spoke of sacrifice and
resurrection. A veteran who had served with Patrick read
from the Book of Wisdom, voice breaking on the words:

"The souls of the righteous are in the hand of
God."

Father Michael's homily was measured, careful. He
spoke of Patrick as a son of Boston, a soldier, a brother
who bore the weight of his oath far from home. He
spoke of courage, of faith, of the mystery of why God's
hand sometimes seemed to fall too soon. His voice
wavered only once, when he looked at Ashlyn and saw
her staring at the Bible in her lap with such fierce
intensity it chilled him.

When the offertory came, incense rolled through the cathedral like fog. The sunlight through stained glass seemed to shimmer unnaturally, colors bleeding across the marble in restless shapes. Father Michael's eyes flicked to the great crucifix suspended above the altar. For a moment, he froze. The shadow of Christ on the cross fell across the wall in sharp silhouette, but at its feet, another shape stirred, something chained, writhing, barely contained in darkness. Father Michael blinked hard, whispered the Sanctus, and forced himself to continue. The Eucharistic Prayer began. Father Michael's voice carried the ancient words:

"Take this, all of you, and eat of it: for this is my Body, which will be given up for you."

As he spoke, a whisper slid across his ear, so close it raised the hair on his neck. Not his voice. Not the choirs.

"Broken faith opens the door."

He faltered, the chalice trembling in his hands. His gaze swept the pews. No one else reacted. Only Ashlyn, clutching Patrick's Bible, seemed to shiver as though she had heard it too. He pressed forward, lips moving, heart hammering. The words sounded hollow against the whisper echoing in his skull.

When Communion was offered, Ashlyn rose with her family. She walked forward, eyes downcast, as she knelt, wafer against her tongue, she thought she heard singing, just behind her, though no one stood there. A voice she knew as well as her own. Patrick. It was not in English. Not Latin. The words were harsh, guttural, yet carried a rhythm like a psalm. Her knees buckled. She caught herself on the rail, trembling. Nora steadied her, whispering,

"You're all right, love. You're all right."

But she wasn't. The Bible in her hands burned hot as coals. The Mass ended with military honor. The soldiers lifted Patrick's casket, the flag snapping tight in their grip. The bugle's mournful Taps echoed against stone. Outside the cathedral, rifles cracked in salute. The folded flag was handed to Nora, who held it against her chest as if it were her son's body itself. Inside, Father Michael knelt before the altar, staring up at the crucifix. His lips moved, but no words came. He had heard something no priest should ever hear at Mass. Somewhere behind him, unseen by all but one girl clutching a soldier's Bible, the air shivered as though chains dragged across stone.

Night

The house was quiet, emptied of mourners and soldiers, their words of condolence lingering like stale incense. Upstairs, Ashlyn lay on her bed, Patrick's Bible resting on her chest. The folded flag sat in the living room, but this, this book, this relic, felt more like him than anything else. She opened it slowly. The photograph of Patrick on the Cape slid into her lap, his grin frozen in the summer sun. Beneath it, the silk-wrapped fragment gleamed faintly in the lamplight. The red Syriac embroidery seemed to shift, curling like smoke, letters rearranging into patterns she couldn't quite read. Her fingertips traced the threads. Heat pulsed through her hand, climbing her arm. She closed her eyes, whispering,

"Patrick?"

Silence at first. Then a sound, soft but unmistakable: a knock, faint and deliberate, from the back of her closet. Ashlyn sat up, breath caught in her throat. She clutched the relic, heart hammering. Another knock, louder this time, three slow raps against the wood, and then his voice, muffled, just on the other side:

"Lyn ... "

The Bible slipped from her hands, hitting the floor. The closet door shuddered.

Chapter 2

A Sunday in Boston

"Cantus populi et vox ludorum eum non obscurant; in templo surgit."
The songs of the people and the voice of games do not hide him; in the temple he rises.

The car smelled faintly of leather and the Dunkin' Donuts coffee Sean had spilled on the console weeks ago. The April sun poured through the windshield, sharp enough that Nora flipped the visor down, rosary beads clicking between her fingers. On the radio, Jerry Remy's familiar voice filled the silence:

"And the Yankees tack on another run here in the eighth, Sheffield with a line drive into left. That'll make it seven to three, New York."

Sean swore under his breath and thumped the steering wheel.

"Every damn time. They had it, too. Thought this year might be different."

Beside him, Ashlyn pressed her forehead to the cool glass of the passenger window. The Red Sox, Yankees, none of it mattered. The Bible lay in her lap, Patrick's Bible, with the silk-wrapped relic hidden inside. She hadn't told them she'd touched it again that morning, hadn't told them how it had burned hotter than yesterday, how the embroidery seemed to shift when she traced the letters. She closed her eyes, and for a moment she heard him again, Patrick's voice, low and close:

"Lyn…"

The nickname curled in her ears.

"Not listening, are you?" Sean muttered.

She blinked. "What?"

"The Sox. Lost again."

"Oh." She forced a small smile.

"Maybe next time."

Her mother glanced back, eyes red from lack of sleep.

"It's just a game. God willing, someday they'll win again, but it's Sunday. Better we think of Mass."

The scoreboard jingle played on the radio, the announcers wrapping up. The Sullivans drove on through South Boston traffic toward the Cathedral of the Holy Cross.

The neighborhood rolled past in sheets of light and shadow, triple-deckers with their porches stacked like hymn stanzas, corner bars propped open to the first warm afternoon, laundry lines lifting to catch a breeze that still carried the bite of winter. A kid on rollerblades slalomed between parked cars, arms out, fearless; two old men at the bus stop argued amiably about the bullpen as if their opinions could turn time back half an inning. A woman pushed a stroller and sang to herself,

some melody without lyrics, and a gull cut the sky with
the rude confidence of a thing that never once paid rent.

Sean kept muttering about the bullpen anyway.

"You can't strand runners like that," he said to
nobody in particular. "You just can't."

The radio faded to commercials, tires, plumbers, a
furniture warehouse promising miracles to credit-
challenged sinners, and then returned with traffic on the
eights. Pike is slow, Expressway worse. Sean took a side
street by instinct, the one that avoided the light at the
corner where the statue of the Sacred Heart watched
over a mural of Larry Bird.

"Shortcut," he announced, as if he were the map's
author.

Ashlyn did not look up. The Bible felt heavier than
it was, as if whatever lay wrapped inside had drunk her
strength. She kept her thumb in the gutter, the way
Patrick used to, habit learned by osmosis from seeing
him with it in camp chairs, on stoops, at the kitchen
table in between shifts and deployments. He had left a
coffee ring on Leviticus. He had written tiny notes
where the onion-skin allowed. She could feel his
presence in the pressure of the pages. When she
breathed, it was as if his breath met hers halfway.

They turned onto Washington Street. The
cathedral's twin towers rose ahead, stone shouldering
sky. For an instant Ashlyn pictured Patrick standing on

those steps in his dress blues, a fade-out memory from
the funeral that didn't belong to this day but insisted
anyway. The sun flared off a windshield; the vision
dissolved.

"Seatbelts,"

Nora said automatically when the car nudged into a
parallel space, and then laughed at herself because they
were already stopped and already buckled. Habit was a
rosary of its own.

They stepped into the afternoon like shipwreck
survivors stepping onto a dock. Sean pocketed the keys,
patted them twice to make sure they were there, and
held the door for Nora and Ashlyn. The air tasted of
exhaust and distant ocean and someone's cigarettes; it
tasted, too, of incense ghosting out the cathedral doors,
a sweet smoke that found the sinuses and stayed.

Inside the narthex, the temperature dropped. Stone
keeps its own calendar. The hush hit the ears like velvet.
Somewhere a baby cooed. Somewhere else a toddler
objected to shoes with the passion of a tiny prophet. An
usher in a name tag that read FRANK handed out
worship aids with the solemnity of a man distributing
secrets. Nora took one and whispered thank you,
because even whispers sound loud in a vestibule.

The air in the nave carried the cool weight of stone
and incense. Sunlight fractured through the stained glass,
painting the floor in colors like shards of glass.

Parishioners filled the pews for the 4 o'clock Mass, families, elderly couples, children tugging at their parents' hands. A woman signed herself at the font with the practiced efficiency of someone late for grace. Two teenagers giggled and then, catching sight of a nun, tried to fold their laughter into piety.

Father Michael Donnelly adjusted his vestments in the sacristy, his fingers brushing the thin metal band on his wrist. The bracelet bore three etched letters: KIA. Killed in Action. It was a small thing, but he wore it for the parishioners who had lost sons overseas. For Patrick Sullivan. For the others whose names he carried in silence. The band had warmed to his skin over the months; sometimes he forgot it until light caught it and memory bit.

He caught his reflection in the sacristy mirror. Thirty-four, Irish-American, Dorchester born and raised. He looked tired, lines deeper than they should be at his age. His mother's face flashed in the mirror for an instant, her eyes hollowed by chemo, her prayers unanswered. He swallowed hard and whispered the old words:

"Lord, I believe. Help my unbelief."

But the doubt lingered, heavy as ever, a coin in the mouth you cannot spit out in polite company. He checked the lectionary ribbon, the cruets, the paten, the pall. He straightened the corporal as if squaring fabric could square a soul. In the corridor a server jingled a bell by accident and winced; Father Michael smiled and said,

"We'll let that count," and the boy grinned, relieved.

The Sullivan family slipped into their pew halfway down on the left. Nora genuflected, touched the wood, the air, her shoulders, as if writing her body into the sentence of the cross. Sean slid in beside her, left enough space for Ashlyn to sit at the aisle, habits of protection making small architecture. Ashlyn kept the Bible clutched against her ribs. The relic burned faintly, a restless pulse. She tried to focus on the organ prelude, the sweep of voices rising around her, but every note twisted, warped by a whisper threading through the music. Latin words. Words she had never studied, yet somehow, she understood:

"Non omnis angelus est lumen."

"Not every angel is light."

The phrase threaded under the swell of the pipes, under the coughs and the shuffling, under the creak of wood that remembers different weights. It ran its finger along the inside of her skull. It did not feel like learning. It felt like remembering something she had no right to know.

Her head throbbed. She pressed her palms against her temples. Nora leaned in.

"Migraine?"

"I'm okay," Ashlyn lied.

At the altar, the candles steadied as if bracing. Father Michael stepped to the altar.

"In the name of the Father, and of the Son, and of the Holy Spirit."

The congregation replied, voices echoing, the great room catching the words and handing them back softer. Father Michael looked out and saw faces that were his to keep for fifty minutes: the man in the third pew who always rolled his shoulders during the Gloria; the widow who wore the same blue coat year-round; the college kid who came late and left early but knelt like a person who knows he is being watched by someone kinder than he deserves. He saw the Sullivans, too, saw Sean's jaw, Nora's rosary, the girl at the aisle clutching a book like a life vest. Something in him tightened, not fear, not yet, but the coiling of attention in a man who has learned to trust the ache behind his eyes.

Ashlyn's breath came fast. The heat from the Bible surged into her chest, up her throat. She heard chains rattling in the rafters. It wasn't a sound so much as a pressure that produced sound, iron on iron very far away. The crucifix above the altar blurred, shadow splitting, as if a second figure tried to occupy the same wood as the first. She blinked and the second figure was gone. A draft touched the back of her neck that no one else felt.

"Brothers and sisters, let us acknowledge our sins…"

Father Michael began, hands extended, the sentence as old as his ordination and older.

When the priest lifted his hands to begin the Kyrie, Ashlyn's body seized. The movement was so sudden the pew squealed. She collapsed sideways into the aisle, Bible tumbling from her grasp. The silk bundle rolled free, flashing red embroidery under the vaulted ceiling.

Gasps rippled through the congregation like wind through wheat. Someone stood too fast and knocked a missalette; someone else whispered seizure in a tone that tried to make sense of what it had no tool for.

"Ashlyn!"

Nora dropped beside her, trying to hold her flailing arms, palms sliding on sweat. Sean swung his legs into the aisle and tried to pin her shoulders, his own face pale and astonished at itself. The usher named Frank half-stood, half-knelt, unsure whether to call 911 or heaven.

Ashlyn's body arched, back stiff as a bowstring. Her mouth opened in a scream that tore through the cathedral: not English, not her own voice, but Latin spat in a guttural cadence.

"Ex tenebris regnum surgit! Fides fracta aperit januam!"

"From the darkness a kingdom rises! Broken faith opens the door!"

The words echoed unnaturally, layered over themselves, as if more than one voice spoke through her. Children began to cry in copycat fear. An old man covered his ears and mouthed a prayer without sound. The organist froze, hands hovering an instant over keys, then withdrew them, letting silence slam down like a lid.

Sean's mind reached for a category and found none that fit the scream happening in the mouth of his fourteen-year-old.

"It's okay, baby," he lied, "it's okay, Ash," and she did not hear him and he did not blame her.

Parishioners backed away, some clutching rosaries, others whispering that it must be a seizure, but Father Michael heard the Latin clear as bells, and his blood froze. The phrases were not random. They were doctrinal in their malice. He hurried down from the altar, gathered his Alb in one hand so he wouldn't step on it, and knelt beside the girl.

Her eyes rolled back, white showing. Foam flecked her lips as she convulsed. Father Michael reached for the words that had never failed him because they were not his to fail.

"Lord Jesus…"

The words caught in his throat. Ashlyn's head snapped toward him with unnatural force, as if a hand beneath her skull had yanked it by the chin. Her lips moved, and yet the voice that came was not hers. It was deep, mocking, familiar in its cruelty:

"You prayed for your mother. She died. Pray for her again, Father. See if He listens."

Father Michael staggered back as though struck, the sound of it in his ears like a slap that had left no mark and all mark. His breath caught, his heart pounding against his ribs. How could she know? How could anything know? The sanctuary light seemed to dim and surge in the span of a blink.

The voice laughed, layered and hollow, a sound that found the rafters and came back thinner and sharper. The laugh mocked not just him but the architecture that held him.

"Ashlyn!" Nora sobbed, tugging at the straps of the book as if it were hurting her daughter.

"Help her, please...Father, please..."

"Give us room," Father Michael said, but his voice sounded like another man's, far away. He forced himself forward again, forced breath into the old phrases.

"In the name of Jesus Christ, leave her be."

Ashlyn screamed again, body shaking until, with sudden violence, she went limp. The transition from storm to slackness made Sean grunt with the physics of it. Her chest heaved, sweat plastering her hair to her face. She lay still in her father's arms, trembling like a leaf.

The church was silent but for Nora's sobbing and the soft clatter of a dropped rosary rolling until the cord snagged. Far back, someone whispered,

"Call an ambulance," and someone else,

"Don't move her neck," and a third,

"Get holy water," as if practical and sacramental might be the same order of help.

Father Michael rose slowly, staring at the Bible on the floor. The silk-wrapped relic lay half-exposed, its embroidery glowing faintly in the dim light, as though alive. The red thread picked at the shadow and made it show itself. He could feel heat radiating from it even from where he stood. He whispered to himself, unheard by anyone else:

"What have we brought into this house of God?"

He bent and, with the caution a man uses to pick up a wounded bird, lifted the Bible and its wrapped heart. He did not touch the silk directly. He slid it back into the cover and pressed the leather shut. His palm tingled anyway.

"Father?" Frank the usher hovered, cellphone in hand. "Ambulance?"

"Yes," Father Michael said, not looking away from the girl.

"And... and some water from the font."

He didn't trust his voice to say holy. The word felt too large in his mouth.

A server sprinted, came back with a small silver bowl sloshing. Father Michael dipped his fingers and let the drops fall on Ashlyn's brow, on the inside of her wrist where a pulse jumped, on the silk bundle hidden under leather. The water beaded and slid and disappeared as if drunk by thirst.

Ashlyn's eyelids fluttered. A sound like a small animal's whine escaped her.

"It's okay," Nora murmured, lying again because love will lie to buy seconds.

"We're here. We're here."

The Mass never finished. Father Michael stood and addressed the congregation with a voice he hoped belonged to a shepherd and not a frightened man.

"We'll pause," he said, ridiculous sentence for the moment's enormity.

"Please pray for this child."

Some bowed their heads at once. Some did it after a second as if needing permission. A few, unsure and unnerved, drifted toward the doors, shame making their footsteps loud on marble. An elderly couple began a halting Hail Mary and the sound knitted others to it, and soon the murmur rolled through the nave, familiar words thrown like a net over unknown water.

Ushers helped the Sullivans carry Ashlyn outside, the crowd parting in fear and awe. The April air hit her face like a cloth. A siren wailed blocks away, then nearer.

A girl from Ashlyn's school stood on the steps with her mouth open and her hands over it, and then she started crying because she didn't know what else a body does when someone it knows becomes a story.

Some whispered prayers, others muttered that it was a fit, an illness, a sign of grief too heavy for a child to bear. A man with a paramedic's calm asked questions with the gentleness of someone who has learned when not to touch.

"Has this happened before? Any history of seizures? Any allergies?"

Nora nodded and shook her head and tried to be useful when usefulness had fled the scene.

But Father Michael knew better. The words she had screamed rang in his ears, written into his bones. Broken faith opens the door. He touched the bracelet on his wrist, the metal cold. He had worn it for Patrick, a symbol of faith in sacrifice. Now it felt like a chain. For the first time in years, Father Michael Donnelly truly feared the shadows inside his church.

He watched the ambulance doors close on Ashlyn's pale face, watched Sean climb in, watched Nora kiss her fingers and press them to the glass, watched the lights strobe the cathedral stone with red, with blue, with red. The siren wound itself up and fled. The crowd's murmur thinned and then thickened as speculation filled the space the siren left.

He stood on the steps with the Bible in his hands
and the silk bundle hot through leather, and the question
came back like a tide that had found a shore it liked:
What have we brought into this house of God?

Behind him, the nave waited, a giant chest newly
aware of its own ribs. Ahead, the street gaped, ordinary
and ravenous. Father Michael turned and went back
inside because that was what priests do when the world
splits: they re-enter the room where it split and begin
again, even if all they can begin with is sweeping. He set
the Bible on the credence table, felt the heat again
through oak, and told himself a sentence he did not yet
fully believe:

"We are not alone."

After the ambulance left, Frank ushered the rest of
the congregation back inside in that Boston way of
pretending normal so that normal will be embarrassed
into returning. Some people sat. Some stood and stared
at the place in the aisle where Ashlyn's body had shaken
the wood. A child reached for a dropped bead and his
mother tugged him back with a hiss that was ninety
percent fear and ten percent habit.

Father Michael returned to the altar and stood,
hands at his sides, the alb suddenly too bright on his
arms. He looked at the crucifix and then down at his
hands and then out at his people.

"We'll finish Evening Prayer," he said finally,
because a Mass broken cannot be mended without
daring a new liturgy.

"God hears every cry," he added, and managed not
to choke on the words.

They prayed the psalms unevenly, as if the
sentences were a floor with boards missing. When they
reached

"Out of the depths I cry to you, O Lord," Father
Michael felt the line land in his chest like a thrown stone.
He pressed on. He preached no homily. He gave no
announcements. He dismissed them with a blessing that
felt like a hand placed on a fevered brow and hoped it
did some small cooling.

In the sacristy afterward, he washed his hands
longer than necessary. The water ran until it went tepid.
He watched a swirl of diluted blood from his palm
thread down the drain and disappear. He dried his hands
on a towel and only then realized he was shaking.

He found the Bible where he had left it and forced
himself to touch the leather. The heat had abated, or else
he had become brave to it. He thought of Patrick's
funeral, the folded flag, the bugle that turns the air in a
human chest into metal sorrow, the young faces
pretending to be old enough to carry a casket. He had
promised himself that day to be the sort of priest who
stayed when the family called at midnight, the sort who

returned to a house after the casserole dishes had been collected and stacked back in cabinets, the sort who refused to put grief on a schedule.

He called Bishop Shaw. He left out the voice that had said Pray for her again. He put the Latin in, the exact phrases. Shaw was quiet on the other end in that deliberate way that signals both thought and respect.

"We will talk tomorrow," the bishop said. "Get some rest if you can.

Rest sounded obscene and necessary. Father Michael said he would try. He did not have to say that sleep for a priest has always been a negotiation.

He walked back into the nave. The light had changed. The blue had deepened in the windows and the red had caught fire. He stood where Ashlyn had fallen and knelt. He did not speak. The quiet in the building felt different now, not benign, not empty; attentive, as if the stone had learned a new language and was trying to hear through it.

In the parking lot, Sean sat behind the wheel of the sedan and could not make his hands unclench. Nora had told him to ride in the ambulance; he had refused because someone had to follow in a car that would not hold a gurney and because driving sometimes is the only choice that looks like action. He stared at the keys in the ignition and counted to ten and back again. He kept seeing her daughter's mouth shape a language school had never taught. He kept hearing her own voice promise it was okay when it was not.

A knock startled him. It was Father Michael, vestments shed, jacket shrugged on without looking. He leaned so he didn't have to roll down the window far.

"I'll meet you at the hospital," he said. "If they let me in, I'll be there."

Sean nodded.

"What was that?" he whispered, more air than sound. "What did she say?"

He could have lied. it was nothing, it was shock. He did not.

"She spoke Latin," he said. "She said that when faith breaks, a door opens."

Nora closed her eyes. "Then we do not break," she said.

He wanted to tell her that faith is not a muscle and cannot be clenched into strength, that sometimes the most faithful thing a body can do is fall apart and be held. Instead, he said,

"We will stand with you."

It felt like a vow laid in the doorway against whatever might try to walk through. On the way to the hospital, the lights turned green with a politeness that felt choreographed. Sean sat in the back of the ambulance with a paramedic who spoke in a tone designed to keep bodies in their bodies. Ashlyn slept the way exhaustion makes sleep look like surrender. The siren, too loud inside the metal, made her eyelids flutter; the medic touched her shoulder and she stilled, that animal stillness that means a body recognizes a hand that intends only help.

At the ER, forms attacked Nora like starlings. She signed her name until it felt like someone else's.

"Any medications?" asked the Nurse.

"No," Nora replied.

"Pregnant?"

"She's fourteen."

"Insurance?"

"Yes."

"Religious preference?"

Nora looked up at that one and had to laugh a little.

"Catholic," she said, "and I would like it to matter."

Father Michael arrived breathless and was directed to a family room with chairs that tried to look like comfort and succeeded at vinyl. He prayed not because he thought God needed a transcript of what he could see down the hall, but because speech kept a human from breaking. He did not ask for a miracle. He asked for mercy. He thought of the line he had heard throw itself around the rafters like a stone in a jar: Broken faith opens the door. He answered it with a line no demon can use against a man: Lord, I am not worthy that You should enter under my roof, but only say the word and my soul shall be healed.

A nurse with a saint's patience came to the door and spoke to Nora and Sean. Words like stable and monitoring and observation moved across their surfaces, buoying them without pretending to be enough. Nora thanked her three times. Sean's, thank you sounded like he had gravel in his throat.

Someone brought coffee in Styrofoam. It tasted like hospital and carbon. They drank it anyway. Midnight pooled in the corners.

Back at the cathedral, the candle in front of the statue of St. Joseph burned lower than it should have; Flavia would cluck in the morning and scold whomever had failed to trim the wick. The building made the small settling noises buildings make when the difference between day heat and night cool argues itself into equilibrium. Somewhere a mouse dared the sacristy. Somewhere a saint in glass watched over dust.

Outside, the air had sharpened. He stood on the steps again with the Bible in his bag, the silk bundle hotter than he wanted to admit, and the city reaching for Monday.

He touched the bracelet on his wrist as if it were a bellpull to Heaven.

"Patrick," he said under his breath to nobody and to the One who counts sparrows and brothers, "watch your sister," and then he laughed at himself, gentle, because theology would have notes about his sentence and God would not.

He started down the steps. The shadows pooled along the sidewalk looked like nothing but absence of light. He had always believed that. Tonight, for the first time in years, he believed they might also be crowded.

Chapter 3

The House on O'Reilly Street

"In domibus lugentium facilius intrat; luctus est janua."
Into the houses of the grieving, he enters more easily;
mourning is the door.

The Sullivans' triple-decker on O'Reilly Street had
always been noisy on Sundays: the television tuned to
Sox highlights, Sean shouting from the porch, Nora
clattering in the kitchen while Ashlyn complained about
homework. The kind of domestic din that filled the gaps
in life with ordinary sound, even if it sometimes grated.

Now the house felt different. As if every wall leaned
in, listening. As if the laughter and arguments that once
filled it had been driven out, leaving a hollow that
something else rushed to occupy.

They carried Ashlyn up the narrow staircase early
that morning, neighbors peeking from curtains as
though tragedy were contagious. Nora cradled her
daughter's head as Sean lifted her under the knees, the
girl's limp body swaying between them like a broken
doll. She was breathing, steady but shallow, and that
steadiness was the only reason they could move her at
all.

Her room still smelled faintly of lilac spray from the
morning. Posters lined the walls, half movie stars, half

saints, colliding aesthetics of adolescence and faith. Patrick's Bible sat on her nightstand, its leather cover dark and worn, the silk-wrapped relic peeking out from between the pages like a tongue. Sean eyed it as though it might move on its own.

They laid Ashlyn down, smoothed the sheets, and sat vigil. Around midnight, her eyelids fluttered open. She blinked in confusion, pale but present.

"I just... fainted," she whispered. Her voice was thin but recognizable.

Nora kissed her cheek, brushing damp hair back.

"It's grief, love. You've been through too much. Rest now."

Sean said nothing. His eyes kept flicking toward the Bible. The silence was heavy, broken only by Ashlyn's uneven breaths.

For a few hours, the house was calm.

By dawn, that calm had shattered.

Monday – The Screams

Nora awoke to a scream that tore her from sleep like a knife. She stumbled down the hall barefoot, heart hammering, rosary clutched so tightly in her fist the beads left imprints.

Ashlyn writhed in her bed, muscles taut, sheets twisted around her arms and legs. Her small frame moved with impossible force, back arched so far Nora thought her spine might snap.

The sound pouring from her mouth was not English. Harsh syllables rolled out, guttural and ancient, a rhythm that vibrated the glass panes of the window.

Sean rushed in, hair unkempt, shirt half-buttoned.

"Ash! Jesus"

He lunged to hold her down, but when he grasped her wrists, she threw him back with a violent jerk. He slammed against the wall, shoulder hitting plaster with a crack. He cried out, clutching the arm as pain flared white-hot.

"Christ almighty!" he gasped.

Nora dropped to her knees beside the bed, rosary beads rattling.

"Hail Mary, full of grace…" she prayed, words tumbling over each other in panic.

But Ashlyn's voice only grew louder, drowning her mother's prayer. Her head whipped side to side, hair lashing across her face. Her eyes rolled back, whites glowing in the dim morning light.

The dresser shook. The lamp toppled. The whole room seemed to vibrate with her cries. Then silence. Ashlyn slumped suddenly, as if cut loose from a string. Her breathing slowed to an exhausted rhythm, sweat plastering her hair to her forehead. Nora dared to touch her, pressing a trembling palm to her cheek. Still warm.

Still alive. Sean leaned against the doorframe, shoulder throbbing, face pale. He whispered hoarsely,

"That wasn't her voice."

The walls seemed to hold the echo of it, low and terrible, long after the girl had gone still.

Tuesday – Boston Children's

The hospital smelled of antiseptic and despair. Bright murals of cartoon animals lined the corridors, but the cheerful paint couldn't disguise the metallic tang of blood and the constant hum of machines.

Doctors descended on Ashlyn with clipboards and gloved hands. They drew blood, scanned her head, threaded wires across her scalp until she looked like a fragile marionette.

"She may be experiencing seizure activity, a young resident explained to Nora, his tone soothing but rehearsed.

Sometimes trauma manifests neurologically."

Sean sat hunched in a plastic chair, arm in a sling, eyes dark.

"She threw me across the room," he said flatly. "Does trauma do that?"

The resident faltered, glancing at his clipboard.

"Extreme stress can release adrenaline. Hysterical strength isn't unheard of."

Sean barked a bitter laugh.

"Hysterical strength, my ass."

Nora squeezed his knee, silencing him. She stared at her daughter's small body in the hospital bed, wires snaking, monitors blinking. She wanted to believe in explanations, in science, but the memory of that guttural voice would not leave her.

On the second night, Ashlyn stirred in her sleep. Her lips moved, breath rasping out words that made the nurse at her bedside stiffen.

"Fides fracta aperit januam."

Her pronunciation was perfect, too perfect for a girl who had never studied Latin.

The nurse, a lapsed Catholic from Dorchester, found herself crossing herself before she realized what she was doing.

By the third night, the doctors admitted they were baffled. The EEG showed spikes, but not consistent with epilepsy. CT scans were clean. Psychiatry suggested conversion disorder, trauma response. Words piled up like sandbags against a flood they could not stop.

Sean exploded in the hallway.

"Conversion disorder? She's not making this up! You saw what she did!"

Nora held him back, tears streaming.

"Please, Sean, please"

Ashlyn lay in the bed, drifting between lucidity and something else. Sometimes she wept and called for her brother. Sometimes she spoke in languages no one recognized. Sometimes she stared at the ceiling as if waiting for instructions.

And once, in the dead of night, a nurse swore she saw Ashlyn smile at the empty corner of the room.

Wednesday – The House Turns

They brought her home because the hospital had no answers left.

The triple-decker felt heavier now, every floorboard groaning as if under invisible weight.

The first night back, the lights flickered. Once, twice, then steadied. Pipes banged even though no water ran. Sean found his toolbox scattered across the basement floor, every tool laid out in neat triangles as though arranged by unseen hands.

Nora woke at three in the morning to a sound that froze her blood.

Patrick's voice.

It drifted down the hallway, soft and low, singing the lullaby he used to hum to Ashlyn when she was small.

Nora's knees buckled. She clawed the banister for support and staggered toward Ashlyn's room.

She pushed the door open.

Ashlyn sat cross-legged on the bed, humming. Her eyes gleamed in the dim light, her smile stretched too wide, her teeth catching shadow.

"Patrick's here," she whispered. "He says the door is open."

The voice was not Ashlyn's. Not entirely. It was layered, deeper, like two voices speaking at once.

Nora slammed the door shut and collapsed against the hallway wall, rosary pressed so tightly into her palm it left welts.

Downstairs, Sean sat in his chair with a bottle of whiskey, staring at the crucifix on the wall. He swore it tilted when he blinked.

And across town, Father Michael Donnelly sat in his rectory, candlelight flickering over open books, the Rituale Romanum, catechisms, even a borrowed neurology text. He told himself it was pastoral research, but the truth pressed harder: he was afraid.

The girl's Latin had been too precise, and the phrase Broken faith opens the door had settled into him like a stone lodged in the lungs.

He rubbed the KIA bracelet until the skin beneath it reddened and burned.

When the phone rang, Nora's voice breaking through sobs, begging him to come, he hesitated only a moment before whispering:

49

"Yes."

Thursday Evening – The Kitchen Table

The house smelled of smoke and incense when Father Michael arrived. Nora had burned frankincense earlier that afternoon, a desperate gift from a neighbor at St. Margaret's. The sweet tang hung in the air, mixing uneasily with the sharper scent of Sean's whiskey and the underlying must of damp wood.

Father Michael paused in the doorway, fingers brushing the KIA bracelet on his wrist. It felt heavier than usual, almost hot.

Ashlyn sat at the kitchen table. Her face was pale, lips dry, eyes sunken with exhaustion. She cradled a mug of tea between trembling hands, the steam curling weakly into the dim light. For a moment, she looked like any sick child.

Father Michael smiled gently. "How are you feeling, Ashlyn?"

Her eyes flicked up. For an instant, there was clarity. "Tired," she whispered, voice barely audible.

He nodded, relieved. "Rest will help."

But then her gaze dropped to his wrist. Her expression shifted.

"You prayed for her."

Father Michael's breath caught. His thumb froze on the bracelet. "Who?"

Ashlyn's lips barely moved. Her voice deepened, mocking, almost gleeful: "Your mother, and she died anyway."

The mug shattered on the tile as Nora shrieked.

Sean slammed his fist on the table. "Stop it!" His knuckles split against the wood.

Ashlyn's head tilted back, her eyes rolling until only white showed. A guttural laugh rolled from her throat, layered and thick, nothing like her own.

Father Michael's hand shook as he traced the Sign of the Cross in the air. The words of blessing stuttered from his lips, fragile, uncertain.

Ashlyn's gaze snapped to him, and the laugh deepened, as though a chorus had joined her.

The Weeks of Decline

Days blurred into one another. The house grew darker even when the sun shone outside, curtains refusing to hold back the gloom.

Some mornings, Ashlyn seemed herself sitting quietly with her mother, clutching a book, even whispering apologies, but at the smallest provocation, her voice would twist into languages no one in the house recognized. Nora heard Latin, Sean thought he caught scraps of Gaelic, and once Father Michael swore he heard Aramaic syllables he hadn't spoken since seminary.

Objects moved on their own. One evening, Sean returned from work to find every family photograph face down on the mantel. Another night, Nora discovered the crucifix in their bedroom flipped upside down, nails bent though neither she nor Sean had touched it.

Ashlyn grew stronger in unnatural ways. At the hospital, two orderlies had struggled to restrain her slight frame, leaving bruises on their arms. At home, she once held Sean's wrists in a grip so unyielding that he swore it felt like iron clamps.

Doctors still visited. Neurologists adjusted medications, psychiatrists muttered about trauma, therapists suggested family counseling. None of it explained the burns that appeared on Ashlyn's palms after she touched Patrick's Bible, or the cold drafts that swept through the house despite sealed windows.

Nora turned to prayer with desperate fervor. Her rosary beads wore thin; her lips cracked from whispered Hail Marys. She sprinkled holy water across Ashlyn's room until the carpet stained.

Sean turned to whiskey. He drank more each night, his voice slurring into curses when Nora begged him to stop. Their marriage, once sturdy in shared grief, frayed under the weight of terror.

Father Michael visited often, though each visit
hollowed him further. Ashlyn or what spoke through her
always targeted him.

"Law school dropout," she sneered one evening.
"You couldn't finish what you started."

"Mama's boy," she whispered another time, voice
so low only he heard. "You prayed and prayed, but she
still begged for morphine."

Father Michael staggered from the house more than
once, gripping his crucifix so tightly it left bruises in his
palm. In his rectory, he dreamed of water rising, of
pounding fists in a confessional. He woke gasping, the
echoes of "You left me in the dark" rattling through his
skull.

The house itself seemed alive now. Lights flickered
in rhythm to Ashlyn's laughter. Doors slammed in
empty rooms. Once, Nora swore she saw writing on the
bathroom mirror: condensation spelling out apertio
before vanishing.

Neighbors began to whisper. Mrs. Callahan from
downstairs knocked one morning, pale and hesitant.

"I hear... noises," she said softly. "Voices at night.
Your girl, she... she's sick?"

"She's fine," Sean snapped, slamming the door.

But as he turned back into the house, a whisper
slipped past his ear: Liar.

The Turning Point

It was three weeks after the incident at Mass.

The day began quietly enough. Nora made tea. Sean sat silent in his chair. Ashlyn slept late, her face peaceful for the first time in days.

But by afternoon, the air grew heavy. The house darkened though the sun still shone outside. The smell of sulfur crept in from nowhere, sharp and acrid, stinging the back of the throat.

Ashlyn collapsed in the living room. Her body convulsed, limbs jerking, eyes rolling back. Sean lunged to hold her, but her strength was monstrous.

"Help me!" he shouted.

Nora dropped to her knees, clutching the silk-wrapped relic. "Take it!" she screamed at Father Michael. "Take it from this house!"

Father Michael hesitated, fear choking him, but the sight of Ashlyn's twisted body spurred him forward. He snatched the relic, heart hammering.

The instant his fingers closed around the silk, fire shot up his arm. He gasped, nearly dropping it, but held on.

A voice slipped into his mind, smooth and venomous: "Your mother begged for you. I listened. He did not."

Father Michael cried out and dropped the relic. It clattered across the floor, rolling until it came to rest at Ashlyn's side.

Her eyes snapped open. They were no longer her eyes, they were black, voids swallowing the dim light.

Her lips parted. From her throat came a hiss like steam escaping a broken pipe:

"Broken faith opens the door."

The television exploded, glass shattering outward. Light bulbs burst in showers of sparks. The crucifix on the wall spun and crashed to the floor.

Sean screamed, trying to hold his daughter down, tears streaming down his face. Nora clutched the rosary so tightly the beads snapped, scattering across the carpet.

Father Michael staggered back, clutching his burning hand. His breath came in ragged gasps, the phrase ringing in his head: Broken faith opens the door.

The house on O'Reilly Street was no longer theirs.

It had become a battlefield.

And Father Michael Donnelly, skeptical priest, realized for the first time that the battle was not just for the girl, but for his own soul.

Chapter 4

Doubt of the Priest

"Umbra Dei non quaerit infidelitatem; quaerit sacerdotem qui dubitat."
The Shadow of God does not seek unbelievers; he seeks the priest who doubts.

Father Michael Donnelly sat in the rectory study at three in the morning, a single lamp spilling yellow light across stacks of open books. Coffee cooled untouched beside his hand. On the desk lay Patrick Sullivan's funeral card, the edges worn from his restless fingers. His Bible was open to the Gospels, but his eyes lingered instead on the Rituale Romanum he had pulled from the parish library. The pages, brittle with age, trembled under his touch. He had read the Latin prayers a dozen times now, lips forming the words softly, but they felt hollow. He thought of Ashlyn. Her voice in the cathedral. You prayed for your mother. She died anyway. His jaw clenched. How could she have known?

Father Michael scribbles in his journal two columns: Illness vs. Evil.

Illness: Seizures. Trauma from Patrick's death. Hysterical strength. Glossolalia (documented in psychiatry).

<u>Evil: Knowledge of his mother. Latin phrases she</u>
<u>never studied. The relic that burned in his hand.</u>
<u>Whispers at Mass.</u>

He stared at the page until the words blurred. His
legal training returned unbidden, argument, counter-
argument. Evidence, witness, credibility. He should have
been a lawyer. Instead, he was a priest, and the case
before him wasn't a trial but a soul. At last, he slammed
the notebook shut and whispered into the empty room:
"God, tell me what this is." Silence answered.

The following afternoon, Father Michael was
summoned downtown to the Chancery, a stately granite
building that had once been a convent. Bishop Leonard
Shaw's office smelled of polished wood and pipe
tobacco. Sunlight caught the glass crucifix on his desk,
casting fractured light on the walls. Shaw himself sat
behind a desk stacked with files, his expression carefully
neutral, the look of a man who had heard more
confessions of scandal than prayers of joy.

"Father Donnelly. Shaw gestured for him to sit.
You look... tired."

Father Michael sank into the chair.

"It's Ashlyn Sullivan, Your Excellency. What
happened at the cathedral, it wasn't illness. I've seen her
since. Doctors can't explain it. The family is falling apart.

I... He hesitated. I don't know what we're dealing with."

Shaw steepled his fingers.

"And what do you think you are dealing with?"

Father Michael swallowed.

"Possession."

The bishop's eyes narrowed.

"That word is not to be used lightly, Father. We live in an age where such talk invites ridicule and lawsuits. The press would devour us."

"I heard her speak Latin she's never learned. She knew details about my..." Father Michael cut himself off, ashamed. Shaw leaned back, gaze sharpening.

"About your mother."

Father Michael stiffened. "How could you know...?"

The bishop's lips curved faintly.

"I read your file when you entered seminary. You are not the first priest to wrestle with unanswered prayer."

Father Michael flushed, anger rising. "So, you knew, and you sent me to comfort a family like the Sullivans with only half the truth?"

"The truth, Shaw said smoothly, is that most cases like this are illness, not evil. Epilepsy. Psychosis. Grief. The Church must be cautious. If we declare every fit a possession, we invite scandal. The Vatican takes such matters very seriously. Quietly."

He slid a folder across the desk. Inside was a letterhead stamped with the seal of the Congregation for the Doctrine of the Faith. The Italian text referenced a division Father Michael had only half-believed existed: the Vatican Exorcism Office, formally known as the Servitium Liberationis.

"This," Shaw said softly, "is what you are asking for, whether you realize it or not."

Father Michael read aloud haltingly. The letter referenced "Umbra Dei" by name. His chest tightened.

"You… you already know what this is." Shaw tapped ash into a crystal tray.

"The Church knows of many names, Father. Most we do not speak aloud. 'Umbra Dei' is among them."

Father Michael's mind reeled. "Then why, why bury it? Why let a child suffer when you have the truth?"

Shaw's voice hardened.

"Because the truth is not always safe. Do you think the faithful would fill the pews if they believed shadows stalked their prayers? Do you think Rome would survive another scandal? Some knowledge must remain hidden. For the good of the flock."

Father Michael stood, hands shaking.

"That girl isn't a flock. She's a child, and something is killing her." Shaw's expression remained calm, but his eyes gleamed.

"Then you had better decide, Father. Are you her shepherd, or a lawyer arguing evidence until she dies?"

That night, Father Michael sat in the empty cathedral, candles flickering along the altar. His voice echoed in the stone as he spoke aloud, though no one was there.

"I don't know what I believe anymore. I see her eyes roll back, I hear her voice, and still I think: seizure, trauma, grief, but then she knows me, knows what I begged for at my mother's deathbed. God, if you are there, why would you let her voice carry my failures? Why would you let this... Umbra Dei... mock Your name in Your house?"

He broke then, shoulders shaking. For a long time, he sat in silence. At last, a whisper drifted through the nave. Not Ashlyn's. Not his own.

"Because you never believed enough to begin with."

Father Michael's head snapped up. The crucifix above the altar cast its shadow long across the floor, longer than the candles could explain.

The next morning, Father Michael returned to Shaw's office.

"I'll do it," he said, voice steady though his stomach roiled. "I'll contact Rome. If they know about this thing, Umbra Dei, then I want every page, every text, every scrap they have."

Shaw studied him.

"It may cost you your priesthood. Once you step into that world, there is no returning to simple parish life. You will see things that will eat at your faith like acid."

Father Michael's jaw tightened.

"My faith is already acid. If it's to be forged into steel, then it will be by fire, not comfort."

Shaw's gaze lingered. At last, he slid another folder across the desk.

"Then God help you, Father Donnelly. Because no one else will."

Father Michael took it. The pages inside were stamped Top Secretum. Latin prayers, fragments from the Liber Obscura, warnings scrawled in margins by priests long dead. One line leapt at him:

Umbra Dei resurget cum Ecclesia ipsa invocat nomen eius.

The Shadow of God will rise when the Church itself calls his name.

Father Michael closed the folder, heart hammering. He knew then that Ashlyn's battle was only the beginning.

Chapter 5

Enter Sister Helena

"Si puerum perdis, umbra ridet; si servas, tunc pugnat."
If you lose the child, the shadow laughs; if you save, then it
fights.

Sister Helena Duarte was born in Mexico City in 1955, the youngest of four children. Her mother sold candles and scapulars outside the Metropolitan Cathedral; her father drove a rattling blue city bus across the crowded streets. Faith was as ordinary as tortillas in the Duarte household. The day began with prayer, and every evening Sister Helena fell asleep to the sound of her mother's whispered rosary. Yet faith was not all she knew.

From the time she was six, Sister Helena often woke in the middle of the night certain someone else was in her room. Her brothers slept across the hall; her sister snored softly beside her, and yet she would see, crouched at the end of her bed, a shape darker than the dark, a figure that seemed carved out of absence. No face, no hands. Only the certainty of presence. When she cried, her brothers teased her, calling her cobarde. Her mother sprinkled holy water, her father muttered that she had too much imagination, but the shadow remained. Once, she told her grandmother. The old woman, half-blind and half-saint in Sister Helena's eyes, pressed a knotted hand to the girl's cheek and whispered,

"Child, when something frightens you, give it a name. Names have power. They can make the terrible small."

So, Sister Helena gave it a name. El Susurro. The Whisper, but naming it did not diminish it. The next time the storm winds shook their tenement, Sister Helena heard a voice inside the thunder, not in her ears but in her thoughts:

"Yes... the Whisper. I am yours."

She never told anyone again. She grew quiet, devout, pouring herself into church duties, into the liturgy her mother so loved, but the memory of El Susurro sat at the edge of her life, like the shadow at the end of her bed.

Novitiate – Oaxaca, 1974

Sister Helena entered the convent at nineteen, to the surprise of her family and the pride of her mother. She studied theology, prayed the hours, scrubbed floors with aching knees. It was a life of order, and she loved it. Until Oaxaca. Her convent sent her south for pastoral work in the villages. There, among adobe chapels and mountains wrapped in cloud, she first witnessed what would shape her forever. A boy of eleven had begun convulsing during Mass, his voice twisting into guttural cries no child could produce. His parents brought him to the convent, begging the sisters for help. The local priest, too terrified to intervene, asked the nuns to pray. Sister Helena stayed with the boy one night. Alone in the candlelit infirmary, she heard him speak, perfect Latin, words she only half understood then: "Umbra Dei." The Shadow of God. Her blood ran cold.

She sprinkled holy water, recited prayers from memory, but the boy only screamed louder, eyes rolling, strength thrashing against the bedframe. Hours later he collapsed, heart seizing. He was gone before dawn. Sister Helena carried his death like a brand. She had failed. Worse, in his last moments, she had heard something familiar beneath his cries, the faintest echo of her childhood Whisper.

Rome – The Servitium Liberationis

In her late twenties, still raw from Oaxaca, Sister Helena requested further training. Her superiors hesitated. Women were not commonly trained for exorcism ministry, but her insistence, her steady faith, and her unnerving experience persuaded them. She was sent to Rome. There she studied with the Servitium Liberationis, the Vatican's exorcism office. The courses were secret, closed, led by Jesuit scholars and Dominican veterans. She learned theology of angels and demons, distinctions between mental illness and possession, protocols for discernment. She memorized the prayers of the Rituale Romanum, studied ancient languages to recognize curses, and trained in vigilance and endurance, but her true education came not in classrooms but in field cases. She assisted senior exorcists in basements, hospitals, rural shrines. She saw children levitate, old men speak in voices not their own, women shriek psalms backward until their throats bled. She saw priests break under the strain.

One night, assisting Father Niccolò, she watched a girl no older than sixteen writhe in chains, eyes black with void. The demon taunted her directly:

"El Susurro."

Sister Helena froze. That was her childhood name for the shadow. The girl could not have known. Afterward, she confessed her terror to Niccolò. He only nodded grimly.

"They know us, Sister Helena. More than we know ourselves."

She bore scars from those years: a slash across her forearm from a restrained victim's broken glass; burns on her hand from a crucifix hurled red-hot by no visible fire, but the deepest scar was still Oaxaca. The boy she could not save.

Failure and Wound – The Lost Child, 1987

By her early thirties, Sister Helena had led minor exorcisms herself, but one case destroyed her confidence. A boy in Naples, possessed after tampering with occult games, grew violent. Sister Helena was assigned to assist. For weeks she prayed over him, but nothing loosened the hold. His parents begged, screamed. One night the boy's body seized so violently that his neck snapped before their eyes. The parents wailed that the Church had killed him. Rome hushed the affair, but Sister Helena carried the weight. She had failed again. That night, she dreamed of the chained figure in the desert. The same one Patrick Sullivan would one day see. The same one whispering:

"Broken faith opens the door."

She considered leaving the order, but Niccolò's words haunted her:

"They know us. They wound us where we bleed. The only answer is to bleed for Christ." So, she stayed. Hardened. Determined.

Present – A Vatican Case

Now, at forty-nine, Sister Helena Duarte carried herself with stern calm. Her hair-streaked gray, her body marked by fasting and discipline, her eyes sharp as blades. She had become one of the Vatican's veterans, dispatched quietly to nations where priests faltered. The case in Rome was an Albanian immigrant girl convulsing in a tenement flat. Sister Helena prayed, sprinkled water, read psalms. The girl screamed in three voices at once, one of them a low whisper Sister Helena had not heard in years. "El Susurro." Her heart chilled. The same presence, circling back after decades, threading itself through the Church's forgotten corners.

When the girl fell silent, Sister Helena knew the battle was not over. The demon had only tasted. Her superior handed her a sealed folder later that week.

"Boston. A child named Sullivan. We have… reasons to believe it is the same."

Sister Helena opened it. Photographs of a fourteen-year-old girl, pale and hollow-eyed. A priest's notes: collapse during Mass, Latin phrases, unnatural strength. A name scribbled in the margins: Umbra Dei. She closed the folder slowly. After all these years, after Oaxaca, after Naples, after Rome, it was the same shadow. The same Whisper. This time, she vowed, it would not win.

Chapter 6

The Demon's Name Unspoken

"Nomen tuum sciet, etiam si numquam dixisti; puerum loqui faciet."
He will know your name, even if you never spoke it; he will make the child speak.

The flight from Rome touched down at Logan under a gray April sky. Rain slicked the runways, making the lights smear into ribbons. Sister Helena Duarte adjusted the strap of her worn leather satchel and stepped into the chill of Boston air. She had been summoned before in her career, Poland, Argentina, Lebanon, but Boston was different. The name scribbled in the folder had already burned into her mind: Sullivan. She whispered it once in Spanish, rolling the sound on her tongue like a prayer.

The Chancery sent a driver; a young seminarian whose nervous chatter filled the silence. He spoke of the Cathedral of the Holy Cross, of the Red Sox game the city still grumbled about, of Boston traffic. Sister Helena barely listened. She watched the drizzle blur the skyline, the Prudential Tower looming above the streets, the churches crouched between. At the Chancery, Bishop Leonard Shaw received her in a paneled office that smelled faintly of pipe smoke. His smile was thin, professional.

"Sister Duarte," he said, extending his hand. "Rome speaks highly of you. Though I admit, I did not expect them to send... you."

Sister Helena's dark eyes narrowed. "A woman?"

Shaw spread his hands. "The Vatican is cautious. Boston is cautious. What happened at the cathedral has already unsettled many."

"And the girl?" Sister Helena asked.

"She is at home. The family refuses hospitalization after... incidents. Father Donnelly has been visiting, but he is... Shaw paused, searching for words. "Uncertain. You will accompany him this evening."

Sister Helena inclined her head. She needed no more words. She had seen uncertainty before.

Father Michael

Father Michael Donnelly waited outside the rectory, collar crooked, eyes hollow from lack of sleep. He had imagined a veteran exorcist would be older, perhaps a Jesuit with white hair and rheumy eyes. Instead, he found Sister Helena Duarte: compact, scarred, gaze steady as iron.

"You are Father Donnelly," she said, not a question.

"Yes."

"You doubt what you saw."

Father Michael bristled.

"I doubt everything. That is what keeps me honest." Sister Helena studied him a moment, then nodded.

"Doubt is not sin, but it can be a door." Her words chilled him.

They drove together to O'Reilly Street, the rain pattering against the windshield. Father Michael tried to explain the situation: Ashlyn's collapse at Mass, the weeks of bizarre behavior, the doctors' bafflement. Sister Helena listened in silence; her rosary beads coiled in her hand like a weapon. When he faltered, admitting that Ashlyn had spoken of his mother, Sister Helena glanced sideways.

"They will always strike where you bleed. Do not let them smell it." Father Michael said nothing. He touched the bracelet on his wrist, Patrick Sullivan's name cold against his skin.

The House on O'Reilly Street

The Sullivan home looked ordinary: a triple-decker with peeling paint, a sagging porch, the flag from Patrick's funeral still draped in the front window, but the moment Sister Helena crossed the threshold, she stopped short. The air was heavy, as if the house itself exhaled. The crucifix in the hall hung crooked, and when Sister Helena reached to straighten it, the wood seared her palm faintly, just enough to make her hiss. Nora Sullivan hurried from the kitchen, eyes wide.

"You must be Sister Duarte." Sister Helena nodded.

"Show me the girl."

Upstairs, the bedroom door stood ajar. Ashlyn sat on the bed, knees drawn up, Bible in her lap. She looked small, fragile, but her eyes flicked up when Sister Helena entered, and something passed through them, a ripple, a gleam too sharp for a child.

"Hello, Ashlyn," Sister Helena said softly. The girl smiled. Not her smile.

"El Susurro."

Father Michael froze. Nora gasped. Sean swore under his breath. Sister Helena's body went rigid. Her childhood nickname. A name she had not spoken aloud in forty years. The girl tilted her head, voice dropping into a whisper.

"The Whisper. I am yours."

Sister Helena stepped closer, forcing calm into her voice.

"You are not her. You are not welcome here."

Ashlyn laughed. The sound was wrong, layered, echoing off the walls though her lips barely moved. The lamp on the dresser flickered, then burst with a sharp pop, glass raining across the floor. Nora shrieked. Sean pulled her back. Father Michael crossed himself, his hand trembling. Sister Helena stood firm.

The room plunged into semi-darkness, lit only by the hallway glow. Shadows lengthened unnaturally, crawling up the walls. Ashlyn's body jerked once, then twice, then flung backward against the headboard. The Bible tumbled to the floor. Her eyes rolled back, and she screamed in Latin:

"Ex tenebris regnum surgit!"

From the closet came a knock. Three slow raps. Then the door creaked open, though no one touched it. Father Michael's breath caught. He had heard that same knocking weeks before in his dreams. The crucifix above the bed twisted on its nail until it hung upside down. Nora sobbed into Sean's chest. Sister Helena moved forward, placing her hand on the girl's brow. Ashlyn's skin burned hot. She hissed, snapping her teeth at the nun's hand like an animal. The whisper came again, clear as a bell:

"Do you remember Oaxaca, Sister Helena? Do you remember the boy?" Sister Helena's jaw tightened. Her scarred hand shook.

"You will not use his name."

The girl shrieked, body convulsing so violently the bedframe groaned. Then, as suddenly as it began, she went limp, chest heaving. Silence. Only the drip-drip of water from the cracked lamp, though no pipes ran above.

Sister Helena stepped back, drawing a slow breath. Her eyes met Father Michael's, and in them he saw both terror and resolve.

"This is no illness," she said.

Father Michael nodded, throat dry.

"Then what is it?"

Sister Helena looked down at the girl, whose lips twitched with the ghost of a smile even in unconsciousness.

"It is what the Church has always feared. The name we do not speak."

Father Michael swallowed hard.

"Umbra Dei."

The girl's eyes snapped open. Black as ink, and she whispered, with Patrick Sullivan's voice:

"Lyn…"

The lights died.

Chapter 7

Darkness in the Rectory

"In aqua mortuos tenet; in confessione voces resonant."
In the water he holds the dead; in the confessional their voices
echo.

The Sullivan home had grown too quiet after
Ashlyn's collapse. Sister Helena and Father Michael
stepped into the night air, both shaken but unwilling to
admit it. Rain had started again, steady on the pavement,
softening the edges of Boston's April chill. They walked
side by side down O'Reilly Street, their breath fogging in
the glow of a single streetlamp. Father Michael broke the
silence first.

"She called you something." Sister Helena's jaw
tightened.

"Yes."

"El Susurro. What does that mean?"

Sister Helena didn't look at him.

"The Whisper. A name I once gave… something,
when I was a child. A foolishness. The demon knows it
because it was there. It has been there all along."

Father Michael stopped walking.

"You're telling me this thing has been… circling
you since childhood? You expect me to believe it's the
same?"

Sister Helena turned, her face lined, scarred, eyes burning steady.

"I don't expect you to believe. I expect you to see. What we faced tonight is not hysteria. Not illness. It is Umbra Dei."

Father Michael exhaled, shaking his head.

"That name again. The bishop mentioned it, obliquely. I found it in those Vatican papers, but it feels like a legend, a shadow stitched into marginal notes."

"That is exactly what it is, Sister Helena said. A shadow. A parasite on faith. The Vatican suppresses its name because to name it is to invite it, but it feeds best when left unspoken, festering in silence. I've seen it before. I failed to drive it out of a boy in Oaxaca. It killed a child in Naples, and now it is here, in your parish, wearing a girl's skin."

Father Michael rubbed the KIA bracelet on his wrist.

"You're saying Rome has known this all along."

Sister Helena's lips pressed tight.

"Rome always knows more than it admits. Protocol dictates that before an exorcism is sanctioned, the case must be investigated thoroughly. Psychiatric evaluations. Medical records. Witness testimony. The Church must protect itself from ridicule."

"Protect itself," Father Michael repeated bitterly. "Not the child."

Sister Helena's gaze sharpened.

"Do not mistake bureaucracy for cowardice. Rome fears scandal because scandal wounds faith, and faith is our only weapon."

Father Michael laughed without humor. "My faith is not a weapon. It's barely a whisper."

Sister Helena stepped closer, her voice low, urgent.

"Then you must forge it. Because Umbra Dei will seize on every doubt, every fracture. It has already scented yours. I saw it in the way she mocked you, your mother. The unanswered prayer, and it will not stop. It will drown you in your own guilt if you let it."

Father Michael looked away, jaw clenched.

"You don't know what you're talking about."

Sister Helena tilted her head.

"Don't I? Tell me, Father, what haunts you in the dark? What door did you leave open?"

Father Michael's hands tightened into fists. He wanted to shout; to tell her she had no right, but her eyes, calm and unflinching, held him like confession, and in that silence, the memory rose whether he wanted it or not.

The Flooded Confessional

It had been six years ago, during Hurricane Irene's sweep up the East Coast. Boston had braced for flooding, streets sandbagged, parishioners evacuated, but Father Michael had stayed. St. Margaret's Church was his parish, his responsibility. He slept in the rectory with a flashlight and bottled water, listening to the wind batter the stained glass, the rain hammering the roof. The power had gone out after midnight. In the thick dark, he had heard it: knock, knock, knock. At first, he thought it was a shutter, loosened by the storm. He rolled over in bed, ignored it. The rain masked all manner of sound, but the knocking came again. Knock. Knock. Knock. Slow. Measured. From inside the church.

Father Michael pulled on his cassock, flashlight beam cutting through the nave. The air was damp, heavy. He traced the sound down the side aisle until he stood before the old wooden confessional, carved oak darkened by years of polish and dust. The door was locked from the outside. Knock. Knock. Knock. He frowned, heart uneasy.

"Hello?"

Silence. He told himself it was nothing, wood swelling in the damp, hinges shifting. The storm rattled everything. So, he turned away. Returned to his bed. Convinced himself it was his imagination. The next morning, when the storm passed, parishioners returned. Father Michael unlocked the confessional to air it out. Inside lay the body of a man. Middle-aged, face drawn, track marks on his arms. An addict who had slipped inside the church before the storm, hiding, perhaps seeking absolution. The floodwaters had risen in the night, seeping into the nave, filling the confessional. The man had drowned trapped in that box.

Father Michael stood frozen, bile rising. He had heard him. He had heard him knocking, begging, and he had done nothing. The police called it tragic. The papers didn't even notice, but Father Michael never forgot the face, pale and bloated, mouth frozen half-open as though in confession. He buried the man quietly, no family to claim him, and he carried the guilt alone.

Return to the Rectory

Father Michael told none of this to Sister Helena as they walked back to the rectory, but the memory gnawed at him, fresh as the day it happened. The rectory was dark when they entered, the rain tapping steady against the windows. Sister Helena lingered by the door.

"Tonight, we rest, she said. Tomorrow, we plan. I will contact Rome again. You pray. You will need more than ritual to survive this."

Father Michael wanted to protest, but the exhaustion in his bones silenced him. He bid her goodnight and retreated to his study. The room smelled of paper and dust. Crucifixes hung on the walls, gifts from parishioners, tokens of his vocation. He sank into his chair, head in his hands. Then came the first sound. A faint creak. He looked up. One crucifix on the far wall tilted. Then another. Then, with a sharp crack, every crucifix in the room wrenched free and clattered to the floor at once. Father Michael shot to his feet, heart hammering. The air turned heavy, pressing against his chest.

On the desk, his Bible rustled as though caught in a breeze. Pages fluttered, riffling faster and faster until they stopped. Open. To the Book of Tobit. Father Michael stared down. His eyes fell on the passage:

"Then Raphael took the gall of the fish, and anointed the man's eyes, and the whiteness scaled away, and he saw."

The words seemed to glow. A whisper drifted through the room, soft, mocking, waterlogged:

"You left me in the dark. You left me in the water."

Father Michael staggered back, hand striking the desk. His lamp flickered. The sound came again, clearer now, from inside the old confessional cabinet he kept in the rectory study as an heirloom. Knock. Knock. Knock. Three measured raps. Father Michael's blood froze. The doors of the confessional rattled. Then slammed open, though no one stood there. From the dark within, a voice emerged, Ashlyn's voice, muffled, as though pressed behind wood.

"Father… forgive me…"

Father Michael's knees buckled. He dropped to the floor, clutching his rosary, words spilling from his lips in broken fragments.

"In the name of the Father, and of the Son..."

Laughter cut him off. A layered sound, child and man, hollow and endless. The Bible slammed shut. The lights went out.

Sister Helena found him an hour later, sitting on the rectory floor amid fallen crucifixes, his rosary tangled in his hands.

"What happened?" she asked sharply.

Father Michael's face was pale, damp with sweat. He lifted trembling hands.

"It... it knows me. It knows everything."

Sister Helena crouched, steady, eyes fierce.

"Of course it does, but listen to me, Father. That knowledge is not power unless you give it to him. Do you understand?"

Father Michael's voice cracked.

"I left a man to drown. In a confessional. Begging. I thought it was storm noise, and now it comes back in her voice..."

Sister Helena gripped his hands, iron strong.

"Then this is your battlefield. Not hers. Yours. If you give in to that guilt, Umbra Dei wins before the prayers even begin."

Father Michael swallowed hard. "And if I can't?"

Sister Helena's expression softened, just slightly. "Then I will fight for you. Until you can."

The crucifixes lay scattered around them. The Bible remained open on the floor, pages crumpled but still glowing faintly with Tobit's words. Faith binds. Broken faith opens the door, and Father Michael knew, with sick certainty, that the door was already open.

Chapter 8

Vatican Threads

"Umbra Dei dormit in chartis; in margine scribit iterum."
The Shadow of God sleeps in pages; in the margins he writes
again.

The night after the crucifixes fell in the rectory,
Father Michael could not sleep. He sat in the sacristy,
hunched over his Bible, its pages still wrinkled from the
night before when it had opened of its own accord to
Tobit. His hands shook as he traced the verse about
Raphael and the fish. Sister Helena found him there at
dawn, kneeling before the darkened altar. She placed a
thermos of bitter Italian coffee on the step beside him.

"You prayed all night," she said.

Father Michael didn't look up. "Prayed, or
bargained."

"Same thing, some days," Sister Helena said,
lowering herself onto the pew. She studied him for a
long moment.

"You heard it again last night."

Father Michael exhaled, a sharp tremor.

"The voice in the confessional. The drowned man.
It said what the girl said at the house, broken faith opens
the door."

Sister Helena leaned forward, elbows on knees.

"That line is not random. It comes from the Liber Obscura."

Father Michael frowned. "The what?"

"The Book of Shadows, Sister Helena said. Her voice dropped as if naming it could draw it near. Fragments of a condemned manuscript. The Vatican keeps what remains locked in the Archivum Secretum. I studied it briefly in Rome, though only under supervision."

Father Michael's throat tightened. "And Ashlyn?"

"Is speaking lines from it. Word for word."

The weight of her statement pressed against the air. Father Michael rubbed his temples.

"Then she's read it. She must have."

Sister Helena shook her head.

"The fragments are guarded. Caged, like venomous snakes. No child in Boston could stumble across them. Which means this: the demon itself is reciting the text."

Father Michael's skin prickled. "So, it's real."

"It is real," Sister Helena said. "And it is dangerous."

Origins of the Forbidden Book

They sat together in the rectory study. Sister Helena spoke, her voice level, as if reciting liturgy.

"The Liber Obscura was never a single book. It began as marginalia; scraps copied in the 13th century by an anonymous Dominican inquisitor. He claimed he was cataloguing the whispers of false angels. Others added to it over centuries. Apocrypha, heretical gospels, exorcism transcripts. A mosaic of shadows."

Father Michael listened, restless.

"And the Church condemned it." He asked.

"In 1312, at the Council of Vienne. Alongside the Templars' documents. The Obscura was declared heretical, but it never died. In the 1600s it surfaced in Spain during the Inquisition. Exorcists noted it could predict manifestations. They swore victims sometimes recited passages they had never seen. In 1611, a Jesuit scribe attempted a translation. His notes became the first exorcism to invoke Umbra Dei by name."

Father Michael felt his stomach knot.

"So, Rome has known of this thing for centuries."

"Yes," Sister Helena said. "And feared it. They call it Codex 114-D, nothing more. Officially it is heretical study material, to be neither destroyed nor circulated, but among exorcists it has a reputation: if the demon speaks your prayer before you do, the Obscura has already read you."

Father Michael stared at the crucifixes still stacked on the floor from last night.

"And Ashlyn spoke my prayer. Before I could."

Sister Helena's eyes narrowed. "Then it has read you."

Father Michael swallowed. "What does it look like, this book?"

Sister Helena's voice softened, reverent and wary.

"Cracked goatskin binding, darkened with smoke. Pages that look blank until lit by flame. Ink that crawls when read aloud. The margins are crowded with contradictions, prayers beside curses, psalms beside heresies. I saw it only once, in a vault beneath Rome. I felt... as if it were watching me."

Father Michael shuddered. "Why not destroy it?"

"They tried. Twice. The last attempt ended in a convent fire. The book remained untouched in the ashes."

Silence stretched between them.

Father Michael said, "So what now?"

Sister Helena tapped her rosary against her palm.

"Now we decide whether Ashlyn's case is a possession or something larger. Because if Umbra Dei is reciting the Obscura, then Boston is not merely hosting a demon. It is hosting prophecy."

Fragments and Prophecies

Sister Helena spread notes across the desk, scraps she had smuggled from Rome, half-burned copies of fragments. Father Michael leaned closer.

She read aloud:

"Non omnis angelus est lumen; quidam lumen abscondunt, et umbram portant."

Not every angel is light; some conceal the light, and carry shadow.

Father Michael rubbed his arms against a chill.

Another line, scribbled sideways in a different hand:

"In ecclesiis dormit; in confessione loquitur."

He sleeps in churches; he speaks in confession.

Father Michael froze.

"The knocking. The drowned man. It was written, centuries before."

Sister Helena nodded grimly. "This is how the Obscura ensnares. It mirrors our wounds, convincing us the shadow has always been beside us."

She turned another page. The ink had bled, smudged into faint black rivers.

"Fides ardens claudit eum; fides fracta aperit januam."

Burning faith binds him; broken faith opens the door.

Father Michael whispered, "She said it. In the cathedral. At the rectory."

Sister Helena met his eyes. "Umbra Dei feeds on fracture. On guilt. It has chosen you as carefully as it has chosen her."

Father Michael leaned back, pressing his palms into his eyes.

"So, what does the book predict? What happens if, if the Shadow rises?"

Sister Helena hesitated, then read the chilling line repeated through the fragments:

"Umbra Dei resurget cum Ecclesia ipsa invocat nomen eius."

The Shadow of God will rise when the Church itself calls his name.

Father Michael exhaled, heart pounding. "And what does that mean?"

"Perhaps nothing," Sister Helena said. "Perhaps everything. Some say it means the moment a priest speaks its name aloud, the demon becomes enthroned. Others say it means a schism in the Church, or war. The Obscura is never clear."

Father Michael looked down at the scarred wood of the desk. "Then what are we supposed to do?"

Sister Helena gathered the fragments carefully.

"Find the missing page. The Folium Obscurum. Rome whispers it contains the only admission of the demon's true nature. Without it, we fight blind."

Father Michael's voice cracked.

"And if we can't find it?"

Sister Helena's eyes were steady, sorrowful.

"Then we fight with faith alone, and pray it is enough."

The Rectory Disturbed

That evening, Father Michael walked Sister Helena through the rectory. She paused often, sensing, listening.

In the hallway, a crucifix rattled against the wall.

In the sacristy, the candle flames leaned all in one direction though no wind blew.

In Father Michael's study, the Bible still lay open where it had fallen the night before. Tobit stared up at them, the verse about Raphael underlined in ash though neither of them had touched it.

Sister Helena whispered, "The book is reaching for you."

Father Michael snapped, "I'm not the one possessed."

"No," Sister Helena said quietly. "But you are the one broken."

Before Father Michael could respond, a sound rose from the confessional in the corner. Slow, deliberate.

Knock. Knock. Knock.

Sister Helena crossed herself. Father Michael backed away, pulse hammering.

From within came Ashlyn's muffled voice: "You left me in the dark. You left me in the water."

The doors rattled violently, then fell still.

Father Michael's knees buckled. Sister Helena caught his arm, steadied him.

"You must not let it define you," she said. "That is how it wins."

But Father Michael could not shake the truth: the words were not wrong. He had left a man to die in the dark.

That night, Sister Helena returned to her guest room. Father Michael sat awake in his study, rosary digging into his hand.

The fragments of the Obscura lay spread across the desk, ink twisting under candlelight, crawling into new words. He stared as letters reformed:

"Non quaeras nomen meum. Vocasti iam."

Do not seek my name. You have already called it.

Father Michael slammed the book shut, heart pounding, but the words burned in his mind.

In the silence, the whisper came again, layered with Ashlyn's voice:

"El Susurro. The Whisper. I am yours."

Father Michael pressed his forehead to the desk. He did not know if he prayed or begged.

And in the shadows of the rectory, the pages of the Liber Obscura shifted restlessly, as though the book itself waited for its turn to speak.

Chapter 9

Archives and Margins

"Umbra Dei dormit in chartis; in margine scribit iterum."
The Shadow of God sleeps in pages; in the margins, he writes
again.
— *Liber Obscura, Fol. Fragmentum 47*

The diocesan archive in Boston was not on any
tourist map. Buried beneath the chancery, the basement
smelled of mildew and candlewax, the air heavy with the
weight of centuries. Rusted filing cabinets stood beside
mahogany chests, parish registers stacked in precarious
towers. Sister Helena led the way, flashlight beam cutting
a narrow path.

"Umbra Dei does not appear in catechisms," she
said. "But in margins. Always margins."

Father Michael followed, uneasy. His collar felt too
tight.

"You think we'll find it here?"

"Rome keeps the Obscura fragments, but dioceses
keep echoes, references, letters, notes of failed rites. We
follow the echoes; we find the shadow."

They descended deeper, past shelves of sacramental
records: baptism ledgers from the 1800s, confirmation
certificates brittle with age. At the end of a narrow aisle,

Sister Helena paused before a locked cabinet. She pulled a key from her satchel.

"Rome instructed Boston to bury these after the Council of Baltimore. Few even know they exist." She turned the key. The lock groaned.

Inside lay a slim ledger bound in cracked vellum. Dust rose as she lifted it free. On the cover: Exorcismi, 1600–1700.

Father Michael's pulse quickened.

They carried the book to a reading desk. Candlelight flickered across its pages as Sister Helena turned them carefully. Names of afflicted scrawled in Latin, lists of parishes, priests' notes.

Then, 1620. Spain.

The entry was cramped, desperate. Sister Helena translated aloud:

"The girl of Segovia, twelve years, seized with voices. The rite attempted thrice. Each time the demon laughed, repeating our prayers before we spoke them. At the final attempt, she cried in the tongue of Rome: Umbra Dei. The Shadow of God. She died in convulsions before the altar. May Christ have mercy."

Father Michael swallowed. "It's the same."

Sister Helena nodded grimly. "The same taunt. The same theft of prayers. It has stalked the Church for four hundred years."

Marginal Notes

Further along, the records grew stranger. Pages crowded with side-notes, contradictory scrawls in different inks.

One read: "Do not repeat the words."

Another: "The girl's eyes burned when Tobit was read."

A third: "Umbra Dei resurget cum Ecclesia ipsa invocat nomen eius."

The same prophecy Sister Helena had recited.

Father Michael's hands trembled as he traced the Latin.

"It knew me, Sister Helena. It used my mother's death, the drowned man in the confessional. Now I see priests before me suffered the same. It devours the wound."

Sister Helena's voice was low.

"Yes. That is its method. It does not break faith with storms or fire. It breaks faith with guilt. The fractured priest, the doubting soul, that is the door."

Father Michael leaned back, pressing his palms into his eyes.

"Then what hope do we have? My faith is already cracked."

Sister Helena looked at him steadily.

"Then you must decide if your fracture will be your weakness, or your weapon."

The Spanish Trail

Sister Helena flipped to a series of letters appended in the margins, written by a Jesuit in Madrid, dated 1621. His Latin was uneven, frantic:

"I have seen the shadow in three children, in one woman. It wears their mouths. It knows our prayers. I attempted the rite with the fish of Tobit, but my words faltered, and the ink on the page shifted under my eyes. The letters crawled. When I woke, three days were gone. The woman dead."

Father Michael shivered.

"Ink crawling. You said the same of the Obscura."

Sister Helena touched the page reverently.

"The fragments of the book bleed into the records. Or perhaps the book itself writes into them. That is why Rome calls it dangerous to even read."

They turned another leaf. An annotation, faint, smudged almost beyond legibility:

"Umbra Dei non dormit; dormit tantum sacerdos."

Umbra Dei does not sleep; only the priest sleeps.

Father Michael's hand clenched. The drowned man's knock echoed in his memory. Knock. Knock. Knock.

"God forgive me," he whispered.

Sister Helena touched his arm.

"You must not confess to it. Save your confession for the altar. Otherwise, you hand it power."

The Page That Wasn't

At the back of the ledger, a page was missing. Torn clean, the stub of its spine ragged.

Father Michael stared at the gap.

"What was here?"

Sister Helena's face tightened.

"Perhaps the Folium Obscurum. The lost page. Rome whispers it traveled across Spain, France, into Boston with the Jesuits. Perhaps it still lies here, mislabeled. Perhaps the demon itself hides it."

Father Michael shook his head.

"So, we're fighting something that's not only in her body, but in history. In ink."

Sister Helena closed the ledger.

"In ink, in guilt, in whispers, and unless we find the missing page, we cannot know its name's full power."

They packed the ledger back into its coffin of vellum and wood. The candles guttered low.

As they left the archive, Father Michael glanced back. For an instant, in the wavering light, he swore the missing page shimmered in the air, faint letters bleeding across stone:

"Fides fracta aperit januam."

He blinked, and it was gone.

Sister Helena placed a hand on his shoulder.

"Next time we meet the girl, we will not only be exorcists. We will be historians of the shadow, and it will know we are close."

Father Michael looked up the stairs, toward the faint glimmer of daylight.

"Then let's pray daylight is enough."

But in his heart, he feared daylight was the shadow's favorite place to hide.

Chapter 10
Ashlyn's Decline

"In ore pueri cantabit, in ore sacerdotis ridebit."
In the mouth of the child, he will sing; in the mouth of the
priest, he will laugh.
— *Liber Obscura, Fragmentum 61*

The Sullivan house no longer sounded like a home. The radio stayed off, the television screen collected dust, and the only voices were whispered arguments behind closed doors.

Ashlyn's room, once plastered with photographs and posters, had been stripped bare. Nora pulled the decorations down after the crucifix on the wall turned itself upside down three times in a single night.

"If it wants shadows," she said, "then we give it nothing to cling to."

But the shadows didn't need posters.

At first, the changes were small. A lamp flickering when Ashlyn entered. Footsteps in the hallway when she was asleep. A scent of sulfur, sharp and choking, lingering on her bedsheets.

Then came the burns.

They began as faint red lines on her arms and back, dismissed as rashes, but by morning they darkened, deepening into welts that curved into unmistakable shapes: inverted crosses, scorched into her skin.

Sean slammed his fists against the bathroom wall the day he found her shoulders marked with three crosses, side by side.

"How do we explain this to doctors? To anyone?"

Nora wept quietly, pressing holy water onto the wounds, but the water hissed on contact, evaporating into steam.

Ashlyn only stared past them, whispering in Latin, the words spilling as naturally as breath.

"Fides fracta aperit januam. Fides fracta aperit januam."

Broken faith opens the door.

Research and Fear

Meanwhile, Father Michael and Sister Helena spent long hours in the rectory library, surrounded by photocopied fragments of the Liber Obscura and brittle diocesan ledgers.

Father Michael's hands shook as he held a page describing a 17th-century boy who had risen six feet into the air during Mass.

"Levitation," he muttered. "They called it 'exaltatio corporalis.' It ended when he snapped every bone in his own arms."

Sister Helena read beside him, lips moving silently. At last, she said,

"It is not levitation for glory. It is levitation for mockery. A parody of ascension."

Father Michael flinched.

"And if Ashlyn…"

"She will," Sister Helena said bluntly. "The pattern is always the same. Speech. Strength. Marks. Then ascent."

Father Michael leaned back, exhausted.

"Her parents are unraveling. I don't know how much more they can endure."

"They must," Sister Helena said, though her eyes betrayed sorrow. "The longer she resists, the more it reveals. Each manifestation teaches us something, but the parents…" She paused. "The parents are the first casualties."

Father Michael looked at her sharply.

"You sound like you've seen it too many times."

Her silence was answer enough.

Ashlyn's Room

Nora insisted Father Michael and Sister Helena see Ashlyn directly. They climbed the stairs together, the air thick and stale.

Ashlyn lay on her bed, wrists bound loosely with cloth to keep her from thrashing. Her face looked hollow, cheekbones sharp against pale skin.

She opened her eyes when they entered.

"El Susurro," she whispered, locking on Sister Helena. The words were soft, almost tender.

Sister Helena's jaw clenched.

Father Michael stepped forward.

"Ashlyn. It's Father Michael. Do you know me?"

Ashlyn's lips twitched into a smile, but when she spoke, the voice that emerged was not hers. It was layered, guttural.

"I know you left him in the water."

Father Michael staggered back.

The bed shuddered. Then, with sudden violence, Ashlyn's body lifted six inches into the air. Her bindings snapped free, cloth fluttering like ribbons.

Nora screamed. Sean lunged forward, but Sister Helena caught his arm.

"Don't touch her," she commanded.

Ashlyn's body rose higher, a full foot, her hair dangling like seaweed. Her arms spread wide, cruciform.

The air crackled. The crucifix above the bed wrenched itself sideways until it pointed downward, inverted.

Then the girl's mouth opened, wider than her jaw should allow, and a scream tore free. The sound was layered her own voice, her brother Patrick's, and something else, ancient and hollow.

Father Michael clutched his ears, but the scream wasn't in his ears. It was inside his skull.

The lamp exploded. Glass rained across the floor.

Ashlyn's body dropped suddenly, striking the mattress with a force that rattled the bedframe. She went still, chest heaving.

On her arms, new burns appeared, smoking faintly, forming two fresh inverted crosses.

Parents Unraveling

Afterward, Nora collapsed against Sister Helena, sobbing.

"She's our little girl. She's just fourteen. Why does God let this happen?"

Sister Helena held her tightly.

"Because the shadow wants to break you, but you must not break. She needs your faith."

Sean, pacing the room, snarled, "Faith? Faith doesn't stop her from burning. Faith doesn't keep her in bed. We need doctors. Real doctors."

"We've tried," Nora said through tears.

"No," Sean snapped. "We tried priests. Doctors don't abandon their patients with riddles and prayers."

Father Michael tried to speak, but Sean rounded on him. "You let her collapse in your church. You let this start!"

Father Michael's chest hollowed. He had no answer.

Sister Helena stepped between them.

"Enough. Your anger feeds it. Your despair feeds it. Do you want your daughter to become its weapon? Then break yourselves apart. Do you want her to survive? Then hold each other."

Her words silenced the room, but only briefly. The cracks in the marriage deepened as the days wore on.

Friends Visit

Nora thought normalcy might help. She invited two of Ashlyn's school friends, Emily and Claire, to visit one Saturday afternoon.

They came hesitantly, clutching homework notebooks like offerings. Their faces lit up briefly when they saw Ashlyn in her bed, pale but smiling faintly.

"Hey," Emily whispered. "We brought notes from class."

Ashlyn tilted her head.

"Notes," she repeated. Her voice was thin.

Claire set a folder on the desk.

"We miss you."

For a moment, Ashlyn seemed touched. Her eyes watered, but then the smile twisted. Her gaze flicked to the crucifix Emily wore around her neck.

Without warning, the chain snapped. The crucifix clattered to the floor.

Emily gasped. "What?"

Ashlyn laughed, but the laugh was not hers. It was deep, male, mocking.

"Children of light. Children of games. Shall we play?"

The lights flickered. The closet door rattled violently.

Claire screamed as the window slammed shut, blinds whipping.

Ashlyn's body convulsed, lifting half a foot off the bed. Her voice shifted, echoing:

"In ore pueri cantabit…"

Sister Helena yanked the girls out of the room, pushing them toward the stairs.

"Out. Now!"

Emily sobbed.

"What's happening to her?"

Sister Helena's voice was iron.

"She is sick in a way medicine cannot touch. Pray for her, and do not come back."

Behind them, Ashlyn's laughter rang down the hallway, followed by the sound of wood splintering.

That night, Sean sat alone in the kitchen, whiskey glass trembling in his hand. From upstairs came the sound of footsteps. Slow. Deliberate.

He froze. Nora was asleep on the couch. Ashlyn was bound in her room.

The footsteps descended the stairs.

"Father Michael?" Sean called, voice cracking.

No answer.

The kitchen light flickered.

Then the refrigerator door creaked open on its own. Inside, the bulb glowed blood-red.

Sean staggered back, crossing himself clumsily.

From upstairs came a scream, Ashlyn's voice, shrill, piercing. Then silence.

He bolted up the stairs, bursting into her room. Ashlyn lay motionless, eyes open, staring at the ceiling. On her chest, burns spelled out two words:

EL SUSURRO.

By the end of the week, the Sullivans were shadows of themselves. Nora prayed without ceasing, lips raw. Sean drank himself into stupors, rage boiling beneath.

Ashlyn drifted between silence and shrieking; her body covered in welts and burns. Sometimes she levitated inches from the mattress. Sometimes she spoke in her dead brother's voice. Sometimes she simply stared, unblinking, for hours.

Father Michael and Sister Helena kept vigil, torn between research and presence. The fragments of the Liber Obscura lay scattered across the rectory table, the same lines repeating like a curse: "Fides fracta aperit januam."

Father Michael whispered to Sister Helena one night,

"She is breaking them. She is breaking all of us."

Sister Helena's face was stone.

"Then we must decide who breaks first, the family, the priest, or the shadow."

Down the street, the Sullivan house groaned under its own weight. Inside, Ashlyn's voice carried softly through the walls, half-song, half-mockery:

"In ore pueri cantabit, in ore sacerdotis ridebit..."

In the mouth of the child, he will sing; in the mouth of the priest, he will laugh.

Chapter 11

Secret Correspondence

*"Umbra Dei non fugiet ad verba ordinaria; ridet et repetit
ea. Sed in Tobit latet clavem, in verbo quod scriptum non fuit."*
The Shadow of God does not flee at ordinary words; he
laughs and repeats them, but in Tobit lies the key, in a word that
was never written.
— *Liber Obscura, Fragmentum 92*

The rectory smelled of candle wax and damp stone.
Father Michael sat hunched at the long oak table,
fragments of the Liber Obscura spread before him like a
battlefield of ink. His eyes ached from sleepless nights.

Sister Helena entered quietly, a thin bundle wrapped
in cloth under her arm. She set it down before him with
deliberate care.

"This," she said, "is not meant to be in Boston, but
Rome has long fingers, and not all fingers obey."

Father Michael unwrapped the bundle. Inside lay a
letter, its paper yellowed, edges crumbling. The ink was
dark but legible, written in looping Latin script. At the
top: Fr. Thomas Dillon, S.J., Seville, 1630.

"Who is he?" Father Michael asked.

"An Irish Jesuit," Sister Helena said. "Born Thomas
Dillon, though his Spanish brethren called him De León.

Scholar of theology, a teacher in Seville and Granada, but he was also a man who encountered Umbra Dei, long before we gave it that name."

Father Michael touched the paper reverently.

"And what did he see?"

Sister Helena's face tightened.

"Enough to know our prayers are useless."

Father Michael's stomach turned cold.

The Jesuit's Voice

Sister Helena began to read aloud, her voice steady, carrying the weight of centuries.

Ad Fratres in Christo. It is with trembling hand that I set to page these observations, for I know not whether ink can contain what shadow inhabits my memory. In Segovia, three winters past, I stood beside Father Ximenes as he performed the Rite upon a child seized by a force we dared not name. The child spoke our words before we uttered them. The child laughed in the voices of the dead. The child rose from the earth, arms spread like Christ mocked, and every prayer fell as straw upon fire.

I tell you, brothers, this adversary is not bound by the formulas of the Church. The Rituale Romanum compels lesser spirits, but this one, repeats and ridicules. It is as if the book itself has been read by him before us.

He knows each syllable, each cadence, as though he composed them.

In my despair, I turned not to Rome but to the margins. Among condemned texts I found a fragment of Tobit, not the one given to us, but a page scratched in Syriac, hidden among apocrypha. Therein was mention not only of fish gall, but of ash, and of words not recorded by the Church. I believe this missing ritual, lost to canon, may hold the key, but it is perilous, for it smells of heresy, and the Holy Office would burn me should they know I seek it.

I write this so that one day, should another face the Shadow of God, he will know: do not trust the prayers you have memorized. They are already his. Seek the lost word of Tobit, else you will perish as did the child of Segovia.

Pray for me, for my eyes have not closed in peace since.

Fr. Thomas Dillon, S.J., Seville, Feast of St. Father Michael, 1630.

The room was silent when Sister Helena finished. The candle flame guttered, as though even fire recoiled.

Father Michael whispered, "He names it. He names it as the Shadow of God."

"Yes," Sister Helena said. "And he claims only a missing ritual, hidden in Tobit, could bind it."

Father Michael leaned back, rubbing his face.

"Tobit again. The fish. The ash. I found that passage open in my Bible after the crucifixes fell. It's no coincidence."

"No," Sister Helena agreed. "It is not coincidence. It is invitation."

Debate of Faith and Fear

Father Michael stood and began to pace.

"If this Jesuit was right, then everything we've been taught, every exorcism prayer, every formula, none of it matters. We're wielding swords against smoke."

Sister Helena watched him carefully.

"Smoke can still suffocate. Words can still wound, but yes, with Umbra Dei, ordinary prayers fail. That is why Rome buries his name. To speak him is to give him stage."

Father Michael slammed his hand on the table.

"Then why hide this letter? Why not teach us? Why let children die in Spain, in Naples, in Boston?"

Sister Helena's voice rose, sharp.

"Because knowledge is a double-edged blade! If every priest believed his prayers useless, faith itself would collapse, and faith is the only fortress we have."

Father Michael shook his head.

"Faith didn't save that addict in the confessional. Faith didn't save my mother. Faith didn't save Patrick Sullivan, and faith won't save Ashlyn."

Sister Helena stood abruptly, face inches from his. Her eyes blazed.

"Then what will? Your clever arguments? Your doubts? Tell me, Father, what binds the Shadow if not belief?"

Father Michael faltered. His voice dropped to a whisper.

"Maybe nothing does."

The silence that followed was heavier than any scream.

The Letter's Margins

Sister Helena spread the letter out under fresh candlelight. In the margins, faint notes appeared, ink so faded it was invisible until heat brought it forth.

Father Michael leaned closer. "What does it say?"

Sister Helena squinted. "'Non repetere verba. Do not repeat the words.'"

Father Michael's throat went dry. "The same warning from the Obscura fragments."

Sister Helena nodded. "Which means Dillon himself copied from it. He knew the danger. If Umbra Dei hears the same word twice, it becomes his."

Father Michael whispered, "Then how do we pray at all?"

Sister Helena's face was grim. "With fire. With improvisation. With faith that cannot be echoed."

Suspense in the Rectory

The candle sputtered. Father Michael glanced toward the corner. The confessional stood silent, but he swore he saw water trickling from its seams.

Sister Helena noticed too. She whispered, "He listens when we read his name."

Father Michael backed away, clutching the letter.

"Then why are we reading at all?"

"Because," Sister Helena said, "if Dillon was right, the only weapon left is hidden in Tobit, and if we do not find it, Ashlyn will not live the month."

As if in response, the flame died, plunging the rectory into blackness, and from the confessional came a single, deliberate knock.

Knock. Knock. Knock.

Father Michael lit another candle with trembling hands. The letter of Thomas Dillon lay open, its ink glistening like wet blood. Sister Helena folded it carefully back into its cloth.

"This is not history. This is instruction, and it tells us: the Folium Obscurum, the missing page, must be found. Without it, we are shouting into the void."

Father Michael looked at the crucifix above the desk. Its shadow stretched unnaturally long.

He whispered, "And if we never find it?"

Sister Helena met his gaze, eyes steel. "Then we improvise. We bleed, and we pray the Shadow has not already written the ending."

Chapter 12

Father Michael's Doubt

"Si nomen tuum dicit, iam te possidet."
If he speaks your name, he already possesses you.
— Liber Obscura, Fragmentum 73

The rectory had grown hostile to Father Michael. Every night the walls seemed to breathe, the wooden beams to shift and groan. Shadows deepened in corners where his lamp could not reach.

He had stopped sleeping in his bed. Instead, he dozed in the rectory study, his chair angled toward the crucifix above his desk. The KIA bracelet cut into his wrist when he curled his hand. Patrick Sullivan's name glinted in the candlelight, a reminder of sacrifice, and failure.

But even the crucifix no longer comforted him. Twice now it had fallen during prayer, the nails bent as though forced from the wall. He had rehung it both times, whispering shaky litanies, but tonight, it seemed heavier than the oak beams that held the roof.

At midnight, the whisper began again.

It was not Ashlyn's voice. It was not the drowned man's voice. It was his mother's.

"Father Michael."

He froze.

"Father Michael, why did you not pray harder? Why did you let me die? I called, and you stayed silent."

His throat closed. He whispered, "That's not her. That's not

The crucifix creaked. The air turned damp. The whisper slid closer, curling into his ear.

"You are a priest without faith. You wear the collar like a thief wears a crown. You pray only for yourself. Even Rome knows. That is why they sent you to this parish, hidden in shame."

Father Michael gripped the armrests, knuckles white. He wanted to cry out, to command it in Christ's name, but the words turned to ash on his tongue.

The whisper grew into a laugh, low and layered.

The Confessional Revisited

Sleep pulled him into memory.

He was back in the storm again, water rising, wind howling against stained glass. The confessional stood before him, its wood swollen with damp. From inside came the frantic knocking.

Knock. Knock. Knock.

"Father!" a voice cried. "Please, Father! I need to confess!"

Father Michael staggered closer. His cassock clung to his skin, heavy with rain.

"Please!" the voice begged. "I took the needle again. I stole from my mother. Father, I don't want to die in this sin!"

Father Michael pressed his hands to his ears.

"I can't, I don't know"

The water surged higher, filling the nave. He saw faces in the flood parishioners, Patrick Sullivan, even his mother all gasping as the tide dragged them under.

The voice in the confessional grew hoarse.

"You left me in the water, Father. You left me in the dark."

The door rattled. Then splintered.

Inside was not the addict but Ashlyn, eyes black, mouth splitting into an inhuman grin.

"You cannot absolve because you do not believe," she whispered. "You never believed."

Father Michael woke with a scream, heart hammering, his chair toppled to the floor. Sweat drenched him.

The crucifix above his desk lay face down.

Crisis of Faith

He could not face Sister Helena. Not yet.

In the sacristy he knelt before the tabernacle, but the words of prayer would not form. Each Our Father faltered halfway, each Hail Mary trailed into silence.

His journal lay open beside him. The two columns he had written weeks ago stared back: Illness vs. Evil, but now a third column seemed to demand itself: Fraud.

What if it was all fraud?

What if Ashlyn's illness was something unseen but earthly, and he was too cowardly to admit it? What if Patrick's death in Mosul was meaningless, not martyrdom but chance? What if his mother's cancer had been nothing but biology, immune to prayer, and he had wasted his youth kneeling to stone and wood?

He buried his face in his hands.

"Lord, I want to believe. Help my unbelief."

But no comfort came. Only silence.

Then the whisper again:

"There is no Lord here. Only silence. Only shadow. Only you."

Father Michael slammed his journal shut. He wanted to run. To walk out of the rectory, down the streets of Boston, and never look back. To abandon Ashlyn to doctors, to Sister Helena, to anyone but himself. He wanted freedom from the collar, from the weight of his failures.

He even imagined it: himself on a bus, collar stuffed in his pocket, disappearing into anonymity.

The thought almost felt like relief.

The Temptation

That night, he dreamed again.

He was back at the Sullivan house. Ashlyn sat on her bed, but she was calm, smiling, unmarked. She looked like the girl he remembered before this nightmare.

"See?" she said gently. "I'm fine. You don't need to fight anymore."

Father Michael stepped closer. "Ashlyn?"

"Go, Father. Leave Boston. Leave me. It's not your burden. It never was. You don't even believe, not really. Why fight for what you don't believe?"

Her voice softened into his mother's.

"You could have been a lawyer, Father Michael. You would have been good at it. You don't belong in vestments. Take off the collar. Come home."

His knees buckled. Tears stung his eyes.

Then the smile twisted. Ashlyn's lips split unnaturally wide. Her eyes turned black.

"Come home," she hissed. "To me."

Hands erupted from beneath the bed, clawing at his ankles, dragging him downward.

He woke thrashing, tangled in bedsheets.

The crucifix was gone from the wall. Only two bent nails remained.

Sister Helena's Confrontation

The next morning, Sister Helena found him in the kitchen, head buried in his arms.

"You look ready to flee," she said bluntly.

Father Michael didn't answer.

Sister Helena sat opposite him, unwrapping her rosary.

"I know the voice you hear. I know the temptation to abandon. I too have wanted to lay down the fight. After Naples, I nearly left the order. I told myself I had failed, that God had failed me, but hear me: the shadow wants nothing more than for you to walk away."

Father Michael lifted his eyes, hollow.

"What if I already have? What if I've been walking away since the day my mother died?"

Sister Helena leaned forward.

"Then turn back. Even now. Doubt is not the end of faith, Father. It is the forge."

Father Michael whispered, "And if I can't?"

Sister Helena's voice was iron. "Then I will fight for you until you can."

That night, Father Michael sat again in his study, journal open, pen poised.

He wrote one line: "Do I believe?"

He stared at the words until they blurred.

Then, faintly, from the confessional:

Knock. Knock. Knock.

Father Michael rose slowly. The crucifix lay on the floor, its wooden Christ face down.

From within the box, Ashlyn's muffled voice whispered:

"You left me in the water. You will leave me again."

Father Michael pressed his forehead to the door. His voice cracked.

"Not this time. Not this time."

The whisper chuckled.

"We shall see."

The study went dark.

Chapter 13

Historical Echoes

"Ex aqua surgit, ex cinere spirat. Sanguine scribit, et sanguis non delet."
From water he rises, from ash he breathes. He writes in blood, and blood does not erase.
— *Liber Obscura, Fragmentum 104*

The diocesan archive had become their second home. Dust clung to their cassocks, candlelight bruised their eyes, and the smell of mildew embedded itself into their skin. Father Michael sometimes thought they had been buried alive beneath Boston, prisoners of parchment.

On this particular night, Sister Helena unearthed a bound volume unlike the rest. Its spine was reinforced with iron clamps, the cover scorched as though rescued from fire. On the front was stamped one word in faded Latin: Processus.

Father Michael leaned close.

"What is it?"

"Transcripts," Sister Helena said softly. "From the Spanish Inquisition. Depositions, confessions, exorcisms."

Her fingers traced the blackened leather. "Rome ordered most of these destroyed, but some dioceses hid copies. This one survived."

She opened the volume carefully. The script inside was tight, official, written by notaries recording testimonies. Names of accused heretics filled the margins, alongside accounts of torture, confession, absolution, execution, but deeper in the book, the tone changed.

Father Michael read aloud, haltingly:

"Segovia, Anno Domini 1620. The girl Inés, aged twelve, did convulse with unnatural violence. Her eyes rolled, her tongue spake not her own but that of Rome. She named herself servant of Umbra Dei, which is to say the Shadow of God. When the prayers of the Rituale were spoken, she spoke them first, and laughed. She rose from the ground, body stiff as iron. Three friars held her, yet she cast them off as though they were reeds."

Father Michael swallowed. "It's the same. The same as Ashlyn."

Sister Helena nodded grimly. "Identical."

Further pages contained more testimony: women in Toledo shrieking "Fides fracta aperit januam" until their throats bled. A boy in Granada who spat scripture backward. A priest in Córdoba who slit his own wrists after hearing his sins shouted in the child's voice.

At the bottom of one page, nearly hidden in the gutter of the spine, a marginal note caught Father Michael's eye. The ink was rusty, smeared.

He whispered, "Sister Helena… this looks like blood."

Sister Helena leaned closer. Indeed, the words had been scrawled hastily in jagged strokes, a different hand from the notaries.

"Oratio non in libro est. In sanguine tantum scribitur."

Sister Helena translated slowly.

"The prayer is not in the book. It is written only in blood."

The candlelight flickered.

Father Michael's stomach knotted.

"What does that mean?"

Sister Helena's lips pressed tight.

"It means someone tried to record the ritual Dillon wrote of, but instead of ink, they used their own blood."

She closed the book abruptly.

"Why?" Father Michael demanded. "Why write in blood?"

"Because ink fades," Sister Helena said. "Blood does not."

Archival Horror

They pressed on, page after page.

One transcript described a possessed friar who claimed:

"Umbra Dei non dormit; dormit tantum sacerdos."

Another noted that the afflicted refused holy water but convulsed at the sight of fish gall, shouting: "Tobias est mendax!"

Sister Helena muttered, "Tobit again. Always Tobit."

Father Michael rubbed his eyes.

"So, Dillon wasn't imagining it. Others saw the same link centuries before."

Sister Helena's hand shook as she turned another page.

This one was different. It was not a transcript but a loose sheet tucked between entries, spattered with something brown. A sketch of a crucifix stood at its center. Beneath, in shaky Latin, was written:

"Si nomen eius dicis, iam aperuisti januam. Si sanguine oras, claudes."

Father Michael read it aloud. "If you speak his name, you have already opened the door. If you pray in blood, you will close it."

Silence thickened the air.

"Superstition," Father Michael muttered, but his voice lacked conviction.

Sister Helena's face was pale. "Or warning. The same warning Dillon gave. The same pattern we see in Ashlyn. This is no superstition. This is history repeating itself."

The flame guttered low.

Father Michael leaned back, exhausted.

"Every page we read convinces me more that we're walking a path already written."

Sister Helena's eyes flicked to the margin note in blood.

"Perhaps that is the point. The Shadow doesn't create. It imitates. It copies. Even our prayers."

"And if he already knows the ending?" Father Michael asked quietly.

Sister Helena closed the book. "Then we must write a different one."

Sister Helena's Breaking Point

That night, after Father Michael had gone to prepare notes, Sister Helena remained in the archive. The candlelight trembled, shadows shifting across the stone walls.

She traced the margins of the transcript, her finger brushing the dried smear of blood.

Her mind drifted unwillingly back to Oaxaca, decades earlier.

The boy. Eleven years old. Convulsing on the cot in the convent infirmary. His voice not his own. His eyes rolling white.

She had tried the prayers she knew, but every line was echoed in mockery. When she whispered Ave Maria, he shrieked it back with laughter.

And then he died.

Sister Helena pressed her palms against her eyes, but the memory surged harder.

The boy's face twisted. His last cry was not his own voice but hers, thrown back at her:

"Save me, Sister Helena! Save me!"

She gasped aloud. The archive air felt suffocating.

Then she heard it.

A child's voice, faint but clear, echoing in the rows of ledgers.

"Save me, Sister Helena."

She spun, candle trembling. "Who's there?"

Silence.

Then again, closer, from the shadows: "Save me, Sister Helena. You failed me."

Her throat tightened.

"No. You are not him. You are not."

The laugh that followed was layered, cruel.

"Oaxaca. Naples. Boston. Always you fail. Always the children die. You do not fight for them. You fight to forgive yourself."

Her knees buckled. She sank against the table, clutching the rosary until the beads cut into her palm.

"Christ protect me…"

The voice pressed closer, right at her ear.

"But He never did, did He? He let you watch. He let you fail. He let me win."

The candle blew out.

Darkness consumed the archive.

In that darkness, Sister Helena saw again the boy in Oaxaca, his eyes black, his mouth wide. He whispered, "El Susurro."

Her own childhood name for the demon.

Her body shook. For the first time in decades, Sister Helena Duarte wanted to flee.

Father Michael Finds Her

Father Michael returned to find her crouched in the dark, candle stub cold beside her.

"Sister Helena!" He knelt, gripping her shoulders. "What happened?"

Her face was pale, her eyes wet. She shook her head. "It knows. It knows what I failed."

Father Michael tightened his grip.

"It's what it does. It uses the wound. You told me that yourself."

She looked at him then, something raw breaking through her iron mask. "And what if the wound is all I am?"

Father Michael shook his head.

"No. You are not your failure. You are the only reason I haven't walked away already. You told me doubt is the forge. Maybe guilt is too."

Her lips trembled. "And if we are both cracked?"

Father Michael managed a bitter smile.

"Then maybe two cracked vessels can still hold water if they lean against each other."

The silence stretched. Then Sister Helena laughed softly not in mirth but relief. "Perhaps."

She lit the candle again. Its flame quivered but held.

They packed the Inquisition volume back into its iron-clamped coffin.

Father Michael whispered, "The prayer written in blood. Do you think it still exists?"

Sister Helena touched the rosary at her throat.

"If it does, it is the Folium Obscurum. The missing page. The lost word of Tobit."

They ascended from the archive into the night air. Boston's streets were quiet, the rain-slick stones glistening.

But Father Michael could not shake the sense that the whisper had followed them up the stairs, slipping from the blood-stained margins into their very breaths.

And Sister Helena, though steadier now, felt the echo of the boy's last cry in Oaxaca still clinging to her ears.

Save me, Sister Helena.

The shadow had found both of their wounds, and it was sharpening them into weapons.

Chapter 14

The Scholar's Help

"Ecclesia est lumen, sed umbra sequitur semper."
The Church is light, but the shadow always follows.
— *Liber Obscura, Fragmentum 118*

The bishop's office in the chancery was a world apart from the Sullivan house of polished oak shelves, a rug thick enough to silence footsteps, sunlight filtered through heavy drapes, but Father Michael felt more dread here than in the rooms where Ashlyn screamed.

Bishop Leonard Shaw sat behind his desk, hands folded. His expression was carefully neutral; a mask honed from decades of diplomacy.

"You've seen what I've seen," Father Michael began. His voice was rough, frayed from sleepless nights. "You know this is no fever or illness. Ashlyn is possessed. The rites are failing. Sister Helena has found historical records. There's something more something the Church has buried."

The bishop raised one hand, silencing him.

"Father Donnelly. You speak of dangerous matters."

Father Michael leaned forward.

"Dangerous for whom? For the child, or for the Church?"

Shaw's eyes flicked upward, sharp as a hawk.

"Mind your tongue."

Sister Helena, seated to Father Michael's right, cut in.

"He is right. There are names for this thing in your own archives. Umbra Dei. The Shadow of God, and we've found evidence of a lost ritual tied to Tobit. Yet the records are incomplete. Where are the missing pages?"

The bishop sighed, steepling his fingers.

"There are… individuals who claim to have seen fragments of such things. Historians. Men who dig too deeply." His gaze hardened. "Men like Elias Kearns."

Father Michael frowned.

"The Boston College professor?"

"Yes," Shaw said curtly. "Once a promising Catholic scholar. He published papers on apocryphal Tobit texts; manuscripts the Vatican would rather remain in darkness. His obsession with exposing the Church cost him dearly. His marriage. His family. His faith. The man has become a thorn in our side."

Sister Helena asked, "Why mention him now?"

The bishop hesitated, then leaned closer.

"Because even a thorn may point the way, but I warn you, he will tell you more than you wish to hear, and he will demand a price: your trust, your ear, perhaps even your soul. The devil does not only mock in the mouth of children. He mocks in the mouths of scholars who believe themselves wiser than the Church."

Father Michael's jaw tightened.

"And yet you bring him to us."

Shaw looked away.

"Because I fear he may be right."

The Scholar at Boston College

Boston College's theology library loomed quiet and cavernous, its Gothic windows stained with late afternoon light. Dust floated in shafts of gold, dancing above rows of manuscripts and microfilm machines.

Father Michael and Sister Helena were led to a corner office stacked floor to ceiling with books. Inside sat Dr. Elias Kearns, gray-haired, stooped, spectacles perched low on his nose. He was scribbling in a notebook, surrounded by piles of photocopied folios.

He looked up, irritation flashing across his face.

"Ah. The collar." His voice was gravelly, his Boston accent softened by years of academia. "And Rome's iron hand." His eyes flicked to Sister Helena.

Father Michael offered a hand.

"Father Michael Donnelly."

Kearns ignored the gesture. His gaze settled on Sister Helena.

"You trained in Rome. I know the look. They send you to sniff out heresy, don't they? To keep men like me in line."

Sister Helena's voice was calm.

"We came because a child is dying."

That stopped him. His eyes narrowed.

"Possession?"

Father Michael hesitated.

"Yes."

Kearns leaned back, lips curling.

"Then the whispers were true. Umbra Dei walks again."

Father Michael's stomach tightened.

"You know the name?"

Kearns snorted.

"Know it? I've traced it through half a dozen languages and four centuries of suppression. A shadow that never dies, always waiting in margins, and Rome" he spat the word "has done everything to keep it quiet."

Sister Helena's eyes flicked to the stacks.

"You believe the missing ritual was suppressed deliberately."

Kearns leaned forward, his spectacles catching the light.

"Not just believe. I know. The Council of Vienne condemned fragments of Tobit in 1312. The Inquisition in Spain buried them again in the 1600s, and when Dillon, your Jesuit, found whispers of the rite, Rome silenced him. His notes vanished. His students sent to distant missions. Convenient, isn't it?"

Father Michael asked, "Why? Why suppress what could save lives?"

Kearns laughed bitterly.

"Because the Church fears power it cannot control. If there is a ritual outside their codified rites, if salvation depends not on Rome but on forgotten words their authority crumbles. Better to let children die than admit they do not hold all the keys."

Father Michael bristled.

"That's blasphemy."

"Blasphemy," Kearns said softly, "is the weapon of the guilty. You want answers? You want the missing page? Then look not to Rome. Look north. To Vermont."

The Charterhouse of the Transfiguration

Father Michael frowned.
"Vermont?"

Kearns rose from his chair, rummaging through a stack until he produced a map. His finger tapped a spot in the Green Mountains.

"The Charterhouse of the Transfiguration. The only Carthusian monastery in North America. Founded in the 1970s, hidden in the woods, cut off from the world. They follow silence, but silence, Father Donnelly, is a perfect place to hide books Rome wishes forgotten."

Sister Helena arched a brow.

"You think the Folium Obscurum is there?"

"I don't think. I know." Kearns pulled another document from the stack: a letter written in shaky Latin, dated 1978, signed by a Carthusian prior.

Father Michael translated aloud.

"We received the folio with the rest of the condemned volumes. It is not safe, but silence is our vow, and silence will guard it."

Sister Helena's eyes darkened.

"So, Rome entrusted it to them."

"Or punished them with it," Kearns said. "Either way, the page lies in Vermont, and if you want it, you will have to break silence older than your own faith."

Father Michael rubbed his temples.

"And you? What do you gain by telling us this?"

Kearns' smile was weary, bitter.

"Vindication. Proof that I was right all along, and perhaps…" His voice faltered. "Perhaps a chance to silence the voice that haunts me."

Father Michael looked at him sharply.

"What voice?"

Kearns' hands trembled. He sank back into his chair.

"My son. He became a priest. We have not spoken in years, but lately… I hear him in my dreams. I see him drowning, burning, dying. The voice says it is my fault. That my obsession killed him." His eyes glistened.

"Umbra Dei has found me too."

The silence in the office pressed heavy.

The Scholar Tested

They left the library after dusk. Outside, the campus was hushed, lamplight casting long shadows.

Father Michael lingered behind, unsettled by Kearns' confession. He turned back toward the office.

Through the window, he saw Kearns alone at his desk, head bowed over the manuscript.

Then the light flickered.

Father Michael froze. In the glass reflection, he saw another figure standing behind Kearns, a tall shadow, featureless, bending low as if whispering in his ear.

Kearns jolted upright, clutching his chest. He stared into the darkness of his office, mouth moving, but no sound carried.

Father Michael ran back inside, but by the time he reached the door, Kearns was alone again, pale and trembling.

"Did you see it?" Father Michael demanded.

Kearns shook his head violently.

"No. No, nothing." But his eyes betrayed him.

Sister Helena stepped close.

"It is already mocking you with your son's voice, isn't it?"

Kearns pressed his palms into his eyes.

"Yes." His whisper cracked. "God help me. Yes."

Back at the rectory, Father Michael laid out the map of Vermont, the Charterhouse circled in ink. The path ahead stretched dark and uncertain.

Sister Helena studied it silently.

"If the Folium is there, we must go, but the Carthusians will not give it easily. Silence is their vow. Breaking it may damn them as surely as possession."

Father Michael said nothing. His mind replayed the image of Kearns, the shadow at his shoulder.

Sister Helena finally spoke.

"Umbra Dei knows we are close. That is why it haunts us harder. That is why it taunts Kearns with his son."

Father Michael whispered, "Then it fears the Folium."

Sister Helena met his gaze, eyes steady despite the storm beneath them.

"Yes. Which means we must find it."

Outside, the bells of Boston College tolled the hour. Their sound seemed hollow, as though swallowed by something vast and unseen.

Chapter 15
The Hunt

"Silentium est custodia; sed in silentio scribitur etiam veritas."
Silence is the guard; but in silence truth is also written.
— *Liber Obscura, Fragmentum 133*

The Sullivan house had become a tomb. Curtains stayed drawn, meals went cold, and the air carried the copper tang of blood.

On a rain-soaked night, Nora awoke to the sound of scraping. At first, she thought it was branches against the siding. Then she realized the sound came from upstairs, from Ashlyn's room.

She climbed the steps barefoot, heart pounding. At the door she hesitated, the scraping louder, punctuated by a low moan.

She pushed the door open.

Ashlyn crouched against the far wall, her fingernails split and bloody. She was dragging them across the plaster, tracing symbols that twisted like knots of smoke.

"Stop!" Nora cried. She rushed forward, grabbing her daughter's wrists, but Ashlyn's strength was monstrous. She wrenched free, slamming her head back against the wall.

The symbol glistened in fresh blood. Its curves were unfamiliar, angular, not random.

Father Michael and Sister Helena arrived moments later, summoned by Nora's screams. Sister Helena froze at the sight of the sigil.

Father Michael whispered, "What is it?"

Sister Helena's face was grave.

"It is not Latin. Not Greek. It is Carthusian."

Father Michael blinked.

"The monks?"

Sister Helena nodded.

"The Charterhouse. I have seen this once before, on the seal of a hidden manuscript smuggled from Spain. Ashlyn has drawn their sign."

Nora sobbed, clutching her daughter.

"She didn't know this. She couldn't know this."

Ashlyn turned her head slowly, eyes rolling white. Her lips parted, voice low and mocking.

"North. Silence. The page sleeps in silence." The candles on the nightstand blew out.

Parents on the Edge

Sean sat at the kitchen table, whiskey untouched before him. His eyes were hollow, rimmed red.

"She's bleeding her hands raw," he muttered. "She's tearing our house apart, and you want me to believe some monks in Vermont hold the cure?"

Father Michael sat across from him.

"It's not belief. It's fact. The sigil is real. The Carthusians live in silence at the foot of Mount Equinox. If Ashlyn knows this, something, or someone, is guiding us."

Nora stood at the sink, wringing a dish towel.

"Divine intervention?"

Sister Helena said softly, "Perhaps. Or perhaps the demon mocks us by pointing to truth. Either way, the direction is the same."

Sean slammed his fist on the table.

"How do we know we're not walking into another trap? How do we know this isn't just another lie?"

Father Michael met his gaze.

"We don't, but if we do nothing, Ashlyn dies."

Silence fell. Rain lashed the windows. Upstairs, Ashlyn sang in Latin, a hymn inverted, her voice echoing as though from a cathedral.

Nora covered her face.

"I can't lose her."

Sister Helena touched her shoulder gently.

"Then trust us. Let us go."

Departure

At dawn, Father Michael packed the trunk of his aging sedan. Candles, vestments, Bibles, Sister Helena's satchel of texts. The sigil had been copied onto parchment, folded carefully.

Nora hugged Sister Helena fiercely.

"Bring her back."

Sister Helena's voice was steady.

"We will."

Sean shook Father Michael's hand reluctantly. His grip was iron, desperate.

"If she dies…" His voice cracked.

Father Michael held his gaze.

"She won't."

But inside, doubt gnawed.

The drive north was long, rain misting against the windshield. The highway gave way to winding mountain roads. Trees loomed close, their branches skeletal against the gray sky.

Sister Helena sat with eyes closed, rosary wound around her fingers. Father Michael glanced at her.

"What if they refuse us?"

"They will refuse," Sister Helena said. "Silence is their vow, but vows break."

Arrival at the Charterhouse

By dusk they reached Vermont. Mount Equinox rose black against the storm-heavy sky, its peak lost in cloud. At its base, in a hollow of forest, stone walls enclosed the Charterhouse of the Transfiguration.

The monastery was stark and massive, built of granite, its towers reaching upward like frozen prayers. No lights shone from the windows. The gate creaked as Father Michael pushed it open.

Inside the courtyard, nineteen monks moved silently, their white habits ghostlike in the gloom. None acknowledged them.

A young monk approached, bowing slightly. His face was pale, eyes downcast. He spoke in a whisper.

"Visitors are not received."

Sister Helena stepped forward.

"We seek the Folium Obscurum. A page you guard. A child is dying."

The monk flinched, glancing toward the cloister. After a pause, he whispered.

"Follow."

He led them through narrow stone corridors to a small chamber where an older monk waited. His beard was silver, his eyes sharp.

"I am Prior Matthias," he said softly. "You speak dangerous words."

Sister Helena held up the parchment copy of Ashlyn's sigil.

"The girl drew this, in her own blood. How could she know it?"

Matthias' eyes widened slightly. He took the parchment, studied it, then handed it back.

"You should not be here," he said. "The vow of silence is our shield, but perhaps silence is broken tonight."

The Forbidden Library

Matthias led them deeper into the monastery, down staircases into the earth. The air grew colder, damp with stone.

At last, they entered a vaulted chamber lined with shelves of manuscripts. Candles flickered, their flames guttering in unseen drafts.

"This is what we guard," Matthias whispered. Contraband texts smuggled from Spain centuries ago. Books the Church condemned, yet could not destroy. We keep them hidden. Not to read. Only to contain."

Sister Helena stepped forward reverently. She traced the spines: cracked goatskin, smoke-darkened leather, bindings stitched with thread black as soot.

"Where is it?" Father Michael asked.

Matthias hesitated, then gestured to a locked case at the far wall. Inside lay a single folio, bound not as a book but as a loose page encased in glass. Its surface shimmered faintly, as if the ink itself moved.

"The Folium Obscurum, Matthias said. His voice shook. Written in blood upon the page. We vowed never to read it. For those who do... do not return the same."

Father Michael stepped closer. The Latin text crawled faintly across the parchment, words twisting like snakes. He felt his heart seize.

Sister Helena whispered, "This is it. Fr. Dillon was right."

The candle nearest the case flickered violently, then went out. From the shadows of the chamber came a low chuckle.

"You think words will save you."

The sound echoed through stone.

Father Michael's hand clenched into a fist.

"We don't just have words. We have faith."

The chuckle deepened into a roar, shaking the shelves.

Prior Matthias fell to his knees, clutching his rosary.

"Go," he whispered hoarsely. Take it. If it saves the child, take it, but know this, once the page is read, silence will never hold again."

Sister Helena lifted the glass case, sliding the folio free. The parchment burned cold in her hands.

Father Michael felt the weight of centuries pressing on his chest.

Together, they turned toward the stairs, carrying the forbidden page.

Behind them, the monks began to chant, voices low and trembling, as if to hold back the shadow that stirred in the walls.

And far away, in Boston, Ashlyn Sullivan laughed in her sleep.

Chapter 16

The Forbidden Manuscript

"In Urbe Roma ipse locutus est per puerum, et Summus
Pontifex lacrimavit."
In the City of Rome he spoke through the child, and the Pope
himself wept.
— *Folium Obscurum, Fragmentum 7*

Boston seemed smaller after Vermont. The
monastery's granite walls, its silence, its chanting monks
still haunted Father Michael's ears. He and Sister Helena
drove in silence, the Folium sealed in Sister Helena's
satchel as though the weight of it threatened to bend the
world.

The Sullivan house loomed dark as they passed.
Curtains drawn, porch light off. Father Michael felt the
pull to stop, to see Ashlyn, but Sister Helena shook her
head.

"Not yet. We cannot face her without the text."

They continued to the rectory. The study was dim,
only a single lamp burning. Sister Helena set the satchel
on the table, her hands trembling slightly as she
unwrapped it.

The Folium Obscurum glistened faintly in the lamplight. The parchment seemed alive, the words curling and shifting, resisting the gaze.

Father Michael swallowed hard.

"How do we even begin?"

Sister Helena hesitated, then said, "We don't. Not alone."

A knock startled them both. Father Michael crossed the study, opened the door. Dr. Elias Kearns stood on the threshold, rain on his coat, spectacles fogged.

"You went to Vermont without me," Kearns said, his voice sharp, but beneath it was relief. "I knew you'd find it. Rome couldn't keep it buried forever."

Father Michael ushered him in.

"We need your help."

Kearns' eyes went to the parchment. For the first time, his cynicism faltered. Awe spread across his face.

"God above."

Sister Helena said flatly, "Don't say His name near this page."

Kearns smirked faintly.

"Superstition."

But when he reached out, his hand trembled.

The First Reading

Kearns set his notebook down, spectacles perched high. He muttered to himself as he traced the text.

"The script is Latin, but not clean. It's layered glosses from scribes, some Syriac marginalia... This isn't a single author. It's centuries of hands."

Father Michael leaned closer. The text seemed to shimmer. One line held still long enough for him to read:

"Umbra Dei apparuit in Hispania, in voce mulieris quae verba in confessione praedixit."

Umbra Dei appeared in Spain, in the voice of a woman who foretold the confessor's words.

Sister Helena's lips tightened.

"That's the Segovia girl."

Kearns nodded.

"Documented in Inquisition transcripts. This is confirmation."

Another line shifted into focus:

"In Neapoli, anno Domini 1582, puer levitavit supra altare. Umbra Dei risit, dicens: 'Ascensio est mea, non vestra.'"

In Naples, in the year of Our Lord 1582, a boy levitated above the altar. Umbra Dei laughed, saying: 'Ascension is mine, not yours.'

Father Michael shivered. It was too close to Ashlyn.

Kearns scribbled furiously.

"These are case studies. A catalogue. Every few decades it emerges, always the same pattern: children, priests, mocked prayers."

Sister Helena asked quietly, "Does it ever say how they stopped it?"

Kearns paused, flipping carefully. His brow furrowed.

"Most end the same way. The victim dies. Or the priest collapses. Or the record ends mid-sentence."

He looked up, eyes dark.

"It doesn't end. That's the horror. It always continues."

Father Michael's chest tightened.

"Then why are we reading it?"

Sister Helena's gaze was steel.

"Because one line, one fragment, may hold the weapon Fr. Dillon believed in."

The Blood Script

As they turned to the final folios, Father Michael noticed something strange. The ink shifted darker, brown-black, with a faint sheen.

Kearns froze.

"This isn't ink. It's blood. Human blood."

Sister Helena crossed herself.

"The prayer written in blood."

The words twisted under their eyes, but slowly they formed into sentences:

"Non verbis ordinatis. Non precibus recitatis. Umbra Dei audit priusquam dicitur. Sed sanguis loquitur quod umbra non potest imitari."

Kearns translated, voice low.

"Not by ordered words. Not by recited prayers. Umbra Dei hears before it is spoken, but blood speaks what shadow cannot imitate."

Father Michael's throat dried.

"A ritual of blood?"

Sister Helena whispered, "Not sacrifice. Witness. Faith written in flesh."

The page seemed to pulse faintly. Letters shimmered like living veins.

Father Michael recoiled.

"This is madness."

Kearns leaned closer, his voice almost reverent.

"Or salvation."

He turned another fragment. The Latin glared up at them:

"Tobias piscem non solum ad demonem, sed ad sanguinem conjunxit. Cinere et igne claudetur janua."

Father Father Michael whispered the translation.

"Tobias joined the fish not only to the demon, but to the blood. With ash and fire the door shall be closed."

150

Sister Helena breathed out slowly.

"This is it. This is the missing piece. Dillon was right."

The candles guttered violently. The crucifix on the wall fell with a crash.

And from the Folium itself, a whisper seeped:

"You read me. I read you."

The Demon Intrudes

The room chilled. Father Michael's breath fogged.

From the shadows, Ashlyn's voice echoed though she was miles away.

"Father Michael. You left him in the water. Now you drown in ink."

The pages fluttered violently though no wind stirred. Kearns tried to hold them down, but his hands shook.

Father Michael shouted, "Get away from it!"

But Kearns' eyes were locked on the text.

"It knows me. It knows my son. His voice broke. God help me, it shows me his face."

Sister Helena grabbed his shoulders.

"Don't listen! It wants your wound!"

Kearns sobbed, tearing his eyes away. The whisper faded, leaving only the faint scratch of words rearranging themselves across the parchment.

One line emerged, stark and final:

"Nomen eius est sussurro. Vocabis et veniet."

His name is the Whisper. Call, and he will come.

Sister Helena's face went white.

"El Susurro. My childhood name. It has carried it for decades."

Father Michael closed the manuscript sharply, slamming it shut. The room fell silent, the air heavy as stone.

They sat in silence, hearts pounding.

Kearns wiped his face, voice raw.

"You can't imagine what I saw. My son bleeding, begging. The page showed me."

Sister Helena said gently, "That is what it does. It wounds through what we love, but now we know its name."

Father Michael looked from one to the other.

"And we know what it fears: blood, ash, fire. Not rote prayers. Not recitations. Faith lived."

Sister Helena placed the Folium back in the satchel.

"This is not history. This is our instruction."

Father Michael whispered, "Then God help us. Because if the shadow already knows our prayers, we'll need more than words to face it."

Kearns' voice cracked, but his eyes held a glimmer of something new. Not cynicism. Not mockery. Something closer to belief.

"Then let's not waste time. The girl is waiting."

The three of them sat in the dim study, the forbidden page between them, as Boston slept uneasily under clouds that seemed too dark for night.

And in her room, Ashlyn clawed at the wall, humming the same words in perfect Latin, as if she too had read the page.

Chapter 17

Demon Unleashed

"Fides ardens claudit eum; fides fracta aperit januam."
Burning faith binds him; broken faith opens the door.
— *Liber Obscura, Fragmentum 121*

The Sullivan house no longer resembled a home.
Furniture was overturned, windows covered with
boards. Crucifixes hung on every wall, though many
dangled askew, chains snapped. The smell of sulfur
clung to the air like rot.

When Father Michael, Sister Helena, and Kearns
arrived, Nora clutched their hands in desperation.

"She hasn't slept in three days. Her skin burns at
holy water. She screams in Latin I can't understand.
Please, please help her."

Sean stood behind her, a man hollowed by grief and
whiskey. His fists trembled as he gripped the doorframe.

"End this. Whatever it takes."

From upstairs came a shriek that rattled the window
glass, followed by a burst of mocking laughter, a man's
voice layered inside a girl's throat.

Kearns flinched.

"It knows we've read the page."

Father Michael swallowed. His collar felt heavy, suffocating, but he forced his voice steady.

"Then we don't waste time."

They climbed the stairs together, entering Ashlyn's room.

She was crouched on her bed, eyes black pits, lips cracked and bloody. Her arms were carved with fresh lines of sigils, written in her own blood. The walls bore the same, symbols crawling like living things across plaster.

When she looked up, her mouth curled into a grin far too wide.

"El Susurro," she hissed. Her voice fractured into three registers at once, child, man, and something hollow, cavernous. "You've brought the scholar. You've brought the priest who doubts. You've brought the nun who failed. Good. Good."

The windows shattered inward in a blast of wind. Glass rained across the room.

Nora screamed, clutching Sean.

Father Michael stepped forward, holding the Folium Obscurum.

"We know your name. We know your pattern."

Ashlyn tilted her head, mocking.

"Then speak, thief of prayers. Speak, and let me echo you."

The Ritual Begins

They formed a circle: Father Michael with the crucifix, Sister Helena with her rosary, Kearns holding the folio, Sean and Nora kneeling by the bed.

Father Michael's voice trembled as he began.

"From the Book of Tobit"

Ashlyn shrieked, cutting him off.

"I know Tobit! I know his fish! I know his ash! Speak, and I will speak first!"

Sister Helena placed her hand on Father Michael's arm.

"Not rote. Improvise. The folio warns: blood and faith, not repetition."

Father Michael nodded, heart hammering. He drew a small blade from his satchel; one he had brought reluctantly. He nicked his palm, blood welling bright red.

Holding his bleeding hand above the girl, he whispered:

"In the name of the God who made flesh, I write with my blood what shadow cannot echo."

Ashlyn's eyes flickered, narrowing. The mockery faltered.

Kearns read from the Folium, voice shaking:

"Non verbis ordinatis… Umbra Dei audit priusquam dicitur. Sed sanguis loquitur quod umbra non potest imitari."

Sister Helena pressed the rosary to Ashlyn's forehead.

"El Susurro, Whisper! I name you!"

Ashlyn convulsed violently, her body arching. Smoke curled from her lips.

Then the laughter returned, deeper than before.

"Name me, and I am closer. Bleed, and I drink."

The bed shook, levitating an inch off the floor. The crucifix on the wall spun upside down.

Father Michael forced his voice louder.

"By the blood of Christ, by the ash of His sacrifice, by the fire of His Spirit, I command"

Ashlyn screamed, a sound so piercing the windows in the hallway burst.

Chaos and Terror

The room erupted. Drawers flew open, books hurled across the space. Lamps shattered. The air smelled of burning hair.

Sean tried to hold Ashlyn's wrists, but she flung him across the room with inhuman force. He slammed into the wall, crumpling.

Nora clung to Sister Helena, sobbing, "Don't let her go!"

Ashlyn levitated fully now, hair streaming upward as if underwater. Her mouth opened, spewing guttural Latin: "Ascensio est mea, non vestra!"

Kearns cried out,

"That's from Naples! It's repeating the records!"

Sister Helena shouted over the din, "Father Michael! Your faith! Now!"

Father Michael raised the crucifix high, blood dripping from his palm onto the floor.

"Shadow of God, you do not belong here! You are bound not by my words, but by His sacrifice!"

For a moment, Ashlyn's body froze midair. Her eyes flickered back to human, tears spilling down her cheeks.

She whispered, "Daddy?"

Sean staggered to his knees. "Ashlyn?"

But then her mouth twisted into a grin, and Umbra Dei's voice thundered through her:

"He left you in the water. He will leave you now."

Father Michael staggered, clutching the crucifix to his chest. His knees buckled.

The floor shook violently. A crack split the plaster ceiling, dust raining down.

The Failure

Sister Helena shouted, "Continue!"

Father Michael forced his trembling voice out:
"Blood speaks what shadow cannot"
But before he finished, Ashlyn shrieked the same words, perfectly echoing him.

The Folium slipped from Kearns' hands, pages fluttering across the room. The words on the parchment crawled, rearranging themselves into mockery:
"You read me. I read you. You bleed; I bleed."

Ashlyn slammed back onto the bed, body convulsing. Her skin seared with fresh burns, inverted crosses etching themselves across her chest.

Sister Helena pressed the rosary harder, but the beads snapped, scattering across the floor.

Nora screamed, clutching at her daughter, but Ashlyn's eyes were black again, lips curling.

"Your blood is not enough. Your faith is cracked. The door is mine."

A gale of wind blasted through the house, extinguishing candles, rattling every wall.

Father Michael dropped to his knees, crucifix clattering from his hand. He gasped, hollow, broken.

Sean roared, charging the bed, but Ashlyn flung him back once more, pinning him against the wall with unseen force. His breath choked.

Sister Helena grabbed Father Michael's shoulders, shaking him.

"Do not give up! She needs you!"

But Father Michael's voice was faint.

"He's right. My faith is cracked."

Ashlyn's laughter roared, layered with voices of children, soldiers, priests. The ritual was broken.

Foreshadowing the Cathedral

At last, the storm subsided. Ashlyn collapsed onto her bed, unconscious, body limp. Smoke curled faintly from her lips.

The house was wrecked. Sean slumped against the wall, blood trickling from his head. Nora knelt by her daughter, rocking back and forth, whispering desperate prayers.

Father Michael sat on the floor, hands trembling, tears streaking his face.

Kearns gathered the scattered pages of the Folium, his voice low.

"It can't be done here. This place is corrupted. It needs hallowed ground."

Sister Helena's jaw tightened.

"The Cathedral of the Holy Cross."

Father Michael looked up, hollow-eyed.

"The place where my faith died?"

Sister Helena met his gaze.

"Then it must be the place where it's reborn."

Silence fell.

Outside, thunder rolled over Boston.

And in the shadows of the Sullivan house, Umbra Dei whispered softly, almost lovingly:

"We will meet again in the temple. There, I will laugh last."

Chapter 18

Aftermath

"Non omnis sanatio est lumen; quidam sunt imitationes ad majorem ruinam."
Not every healing is light; some are imitations for greater ruin.
— *Liber Obscura, Fragmentum 137*

The Sullivan house smelled of smoke and broken plaster. The failed exorcism had left the rooms wrecked: shattered glass in the hallway, crucifixes hanging crooked, sigils smeared in blood across the walls.

Nora sat beside Ashlyn's bed, stroking her daughter's hair. Ashlyn lay unconscious, her chest rising and falling unevenly. Every so often her lips twitched, whispering fragments of Latin.

Sean paced like a caged animal, his fists clenched, jaw tight.

"You said you could stop this. You said the Church had prayers." His voice cracked into a growl. "And now look at her. She's worse."

Father Michael sat slumped in a chair, hollow-eyed, unable to answer. His hands still bore the dried blood of the ritual; the crucifix lay bent beside his chair.

Sister Helena stood in the corner, her rosary snapped, beads scattered across the floor. She gathered them one by one, her expression unreadable.

Dr. Kearns scribbled notes at the desk, his spectacles low on his nose. His voice was flat, clinical. "The Folium was clear. Ordinary words fail. The blood ritual came closer, but it wasn't enough. Faith is the missing piece."

Sean whirled on him.

"Faith? My daughter is bleeding herself dry on these walls, and you're scribbling theories!" He pointed to Father Michael. "And him, he can barely stand. What kind of priest doubts when a child needs saving?"

Father Michael flinched, his stomach hollowing out.

Sister Helena intervened sharply.

"Enough. Blame will not free her. Silence will."

The words cut through the room. Sean turned away, trembling.

The house fell quiet except for Ashlyn's shallow breaths. The air felt heavier than stone, like the shadow itself was crouched in every corner.

Sister Helena's Confession

Later that night, after Sean and Nora had drifted into exhausted half-sleep on the couch, Sister Helena found Father Michael in the kitchen. The crucifix dangled from his hand; his gaze fixed on the floor.

She set her beads gently on the table.

"You think you are alone in failure."

Father Michael didn't look up.

"Aren't I? I broke. He mocked me, echoed every word."

Sister Helena's voice was low.

"Then hear my failure. Perhaps it will teach you that doubt does not make you less. It makes you human."

Father Michael finally raised his eyes. Her face was tired, lined by shadows.

She began.

"When I was still young in the convent, I was sent to a village in Oaxaca. A boy lay sick, wasting away. His family begged for prayer. I was fervent, naive. I knelt at his bedside all night, whispering psalms, crying out for healing."

Her hands tightened on the rosary.

"The next morning, he was better. His fever broke. He sat up. The village rejoiced. They said it was a miracle, that Sister Helena had called heaven to earth. My reputation soared."

Father Michael frowned. "But...?"

Her voice broke.

"Three days later, the boy died. Violently. Convulsions so fierce he broke his own bones. His eyes rolled back, his mouth filled with foam. The doctors were baffled, but I knew." She pressed her fist to her chest. "I knew my prayer had not healed him. Something else had answered. Something that imitated the light long enough to make the darkness crueler."

Father Michael's throat went dry.

"Umbra Dei."

Sister Helena nodded, eyes glistening.

"The false miracle. My prayer opened the door. I gave it a chance to mock God, to destroy more completely, and the family... they cursed me. They said I had damned their son."

Silence pressed between them.

Father Michael whispered, "And you carried that alone."

Sister Helena looked away.

"It is why I fight now. Every child is that boy. Every scream is his. If I can save one, perhaps the shadow will not have the last word."

Father Michael leaned forward.

"And if we fail again?"

Her gaze steadied.

"Then we rise again. Doubt and guilt are our wounds, but they are also what make us dangerous. Because we know what failure costs, and we refuse to let it win twice."

Father Michael felt something shift inside him, not yet belief, but a spark. A refusal.

Parents in Despair

In the living room, Nora sat beside Ashlyn's bed, her hands clasped so tightly her knuckles bled white.

"She's just a girl," she whispered. "Fourteen. She should be worrying about school dances, not demons."

Sean stood by the window, staring into the rain.

"If this fails again... if she dies..." His voice trailed off.

Nora turned sharply.

"Don't say it."

But Sean shook his head.

"She called my name tonight, Nora. For a moment, she was there. Then it laughed through her. I don't know how much more I can take."

Nora clutched his hand.

"Then hold on. Even if you hate the Church, even if you hate them, hold on for her."

Tears ran down Sean' cheeks. He nodded, but his shoulders sagged with defeat.

From upstairs came a faint humming, Ashlyn's voice, soft, almost melodic. Nora stiffened.

The tune was familiar. A lullaby she used to sing when Ashlyn was a baby.

But the words were wrong.

In Latin, the girl whispered: "Dormit Ecclesia, et ego vigil."

The Church sleeps, and I keep watch.

Sean slammed his fist into the wall, fury breaking through despair.

"It's mocking even that. Even her childhood."

Nora clutched him, both trembling, both broken.

Father Michael's Dream

That night, Father Michael dozed fitfully in the rectory study. The crucifix lay across his chest, the Folium sat locked in its satchel.

Sleep pulled him under.

He stood in the Cathedral of the Holy Cross, sunlight streaming through stained glass. The air was warm, filled with incense. At the altar stood an angel, radiant, its wings white fire.

"Father Michael," it said, voice like a choir. "You have suffered long. You have doubted long. Let me ease your burden."

Father Michael fell to his knees, tears spilling.

"Are you real?"

The angel smiled.

"I am certainty. I am the answer you begged for when your mother died. I am the voice you longed to hear in the confessional when the addict drowned. I am what Rome hides and what your prayers failed to bring."

Father Michael reached out, trembling.

"Then tell me how to save her. Tell me how to win."

The angel's smile widened.

"You cannot. You were never meant to. Leave the girl. Walk away. Your faith will be restored when you abandon this fight. Certainty is yours, if you let her die."

Father Michael froze, horror sinking in. The angel's face shifted, radiant features melting into shadow. The wings curled into smoke.

Umbra Dei leaned close, whispering in the addict's drowned voice: "You left me in the water. Leave her now. Be free."

Father Michael screamed, clutching the crucifix.

He woke with a start, sweat pouring down his face, lungs burning.

The crucifix lay on the floor, snapped in half.

Father Michael stumbled into the kitchen. Sister Helena sat at the table, rosary repaired, eyes heavy.

"You saw him too," she said softly, as if she already knew.

Father Michael nodded, trembling.

"He came as an angel. He offered me certainty if I abandoned her."

Sister Helena's eyes hardened.

"Then we know we are close. He tempts hardest before he breaks."

Father Michael gripped the table, breath ragged.

"What if I do abandon her?"

Sister Helena's voice was steel.

"Then I will not, and neither will Kearns, and neither will her parents. You are not alone, Father Michael. Even if you think you are."

Father Michael closed his eyes, the words sinking deep. For the first time, he believed them.

Outside, dawn broke faintly through rainclouds. The Cathedral bells began to toll, distant but clear.

The next battle would not be in this house.

It would be in sacred stone, where faith itself would be tested.

Chapter 19
Preparations

"In ecclesiis dormit; in confessione loquitur. In sanctuario ridet."
He sleeps in churches; in confession he speaks. In the sanctuary he laughs.
— *Liber Obscura, Fragmentum 142*

The Cathedral of the Holy Cross loomed in the South End like a fortress of stone, its spires stabbing the Boston skyline. On ordinary Sundays, its nave echoed with hymns, light filtering through stained glass onto the faithful. Tonight, it was hushed, emptied of pew-sitters, the air heavy with something older than prayer.

Bishop Shaw had grudgingly given permission. The doors were locked, guards posted discreetly outside. To the world, the church was merely closed for the evening. Inside, it became a war-room.

Relics were brought forth from the vault: a silver reliquary containing a fragment of the True Cross, a vial of oil blessed in Rome, a chalice that had survived fires in two centuries. Vestments were laid over the altar, crimson and white. Brass candelabra lined the transept, hundreds of beeswax candles dripping steady rivers of wax. The air was thick with frankincense, almost choking in its sweetness.

At the center, before the altar, they placed a heavy wooden chair. Restraints were bolted to its arms and legs. This would be Ashlyn's seat.

Father Michael walked slowly down the nave, the echo of his footsteps sharp. His collar felt tighter than ever. He remembered baptisms, funerals, weddings he had performed here, moments of light. Tonight, the church felt like a tomb.

Sister Helena trailed beside him, her expression grave but resolute.

"Every stone here has absorbed prayer for over a century," she said softly. "It will fight with us."

Father Michael wasn't sure. The cathedral was sacred, yes, but Umbra Dei had already laughed in lesser sanctuaries.

At the far doors, the Sullivans entered. Sean carried Ashlyn in his arms, her body thin and trembling. She did not resist. Her eyes were open, black as polished obsidian, but her face wore a calm, unsettling smile.

Father Michael's stomach turned. He almost preferred her screams.

They strapped her gently to the chair. Nora kissed her daughter's forehead, whispering, "Stay with us."

Ashlyn's lips curved.

"I am always with you." The voice was threefold again, child, man, abyss.

Candles guttered despite the still air.

The Cathedral was ready.

The Scholar's Summons

Dr. Kearns stood by the side altar, spectacles in hand, gazing up at the crucifix that towered above the nave. His face was pale. The last time he had stood here, it had been with his wife and young son, years ago, before his faith cracked and fell.

Father Michael approached.

"You said you had someone."

Kearns nodded grimly.

"My son. Father Daniel Kearns. He serves at St. Ignatius, just across town. He... he won't want to see me, but he may be the strength we need."

Sister Helena arched a brow.

"You trust him to stand against Umbra Dei?"

Kearns' voice trembled.

"He believes in what I no longer could. Perhaps his faith can shore up where mine failed."

Father Michael put a hand on his shoulder.

"Call him."

The phone call was short, awkward, filled with pauses. Daniel's voice was cold, wary, but when Father

Michael explained what they faced, when he said a child's life depends on you, Daniel agreed.

An hour later, the cathedral doors opened. A young priest entered, tall, dark-haired, features hard with suspicion. His Roman collar was crisp, his eyes sharp.

"Father Donnelly," he greeted stiffly. Then his gaze flicked to his father. His jaw tightened.

"You."

Kearns' shoulders sagged.

"Daniel."

The silence stretched.

Father Michael stepped between them.

"Whatever lies between you must wait. There is a demon here, and it will use your hatred to break us."

Daniel's eyes lingered on his father. At last, he gave a curt nod.

"Very well. I will serve the girl, but when this is done" He left the sentence unfinished.

Sister Helena handed him a small vial of holy water.

"Then begin by blessing what your father cannot."

For the first time, Daniel looked unsettled. He glanced at his father, then accepted the vial. Together, they sprinkled the aisles, chanting prayers.

The estranged pair stood side by side, though a gulf of years stretched between them.

Relics and Shadows

Preparations stretched deep into the night.

Sister Helena arranged relics across the altar: the chalice, the reliquary, the oil. She placed the Folium Obscurum near the pulpit, bound in cloth.

"We use it only if we must," she told Father Michael.

Daniel raised the monstrance, placing it at the center of the sanctuary. The golden rays caught candlelight, casting long spears across the marble floor.

"The Presence will not abandon us," he said firmly.

Kearns muttered under his breath, "It abandoned me."

Daniel froze, glaring.

"Or you abandoned it."

Sister Helena snapped, "Enough. Your quarrel is nothing compared to hers." She gestured at Ashlyn.

The girl sat in silence, watching, her lips moving faintly. Father Michael leaned closer, trying to hear.

She was reciting the Ave Maria, but backward.

Her skin bore fresh burns shaped like thorns, spiraling down her arms. Blood seeped slowly, staining her dress.

Nora sobbed quietly into Sean' shoulder.

"She's slipping away."

Father Michael knelt beside them.

"We will not let go. Not here."

Sean' eyes were glassy.

"This place... it feels heavy. Like she's already won."

Father Michael forced his voice steady.

"Then it's the weight of what we must carry. Nothing less than a cross."

Candles flickered violently. A faint laugh echoed through the vaulted ceiling.

Kearns shuddered.

"It's awake already."

Fault Lines

Tension boiled beneath the preparations.

In the sacristy, Daniel cornered his father.

"You dragged me into this madness to vindicate yourself. Admit it."

Kearns' voice cracked.

"I dragged you because I was wrong to leave. Because I wanted proof that I wasn't insane, and because, God help me, I need you."

Daniel's jaw clenched.

"You broke mother. You broke me."

Kearns swallowed hard.

"Yes, and now a child may die if I don't stand here with you. Hate me later. Tonight, pray beside me."

Daniel's glare softened by a hair.

"You never prayed with me as a boy."

Kearns' eyes glistened.

"Then let me pray with you now."

Daniel said nothing, but he didn't walk away.

Meanwhile, Sister Helena found Father Michael alone in the confessional, staring at the wood paneling. He whispered, "This is where I failed him. The addict. The drowned man. This very box."

Sister Helena touched his arm.

"Then redeem it. Make this the place where your voice does not fail.

Father Michael looked up at her, haunted.

"And if I break again?"

Her eyes were steady.

"Then I will not, and neither will they. We stand together now."

For the first time that night, Father Michael believed it might be true.

The Cathedral stood ready. Relics gleamed in candlelight, incense rose in curls, holy water shimmered in glass. The Sullivan parents knelt in the pews, clutching rosaries until their knuckles went white.

Ashlyn sat restrained, her face pale, her eyes bottomless voids. She hummed a hymn, each note sour, bent, twisted.

Daniel and Kearns stood side by side at the altar, oil and book in hand. Sister Helena tightened the cloth around the Folium, locking it in place. Father Michael held the crucifix aloft, blood from his earlier wound still staining the wood.

The air pressed down, thick, suffocating. Somewhere in the rafters, a laugh echoed, deep, endless.

Umbra Dei was waiting.

Father Michael whispered, "Tonight, we fight again."

The candles guttered once more, as though the Cathedral itself exhaled.

Chapter 20

The First Assault

"Umbra Dei resurget cum Ecclesia ipsa invocat nomen eius."
The Shadow of God will rise when the Church itself calls his
name.
— *Liber Obscura, Fragmentum 88*

The doors of the Cathedral of the Holy Cross shut
like a vault over grave-silence. Iron bolts slid home with
a dull, marrow-deep thud that seemed to echo under the
ribs. Outside, in the damp Spring dark of Boston's South
End, the city kept breathing, cars hissing along
Washington Street, laughter spilling from restaurant
doorways, a siren unfurling down Tremont, yet none of
it seeped into the stone. The cathedral draught
swallowed ordinary sound and exhaled something older.

Candlelight kindled the nave in tiers and islands:
little oceans of flame riding the long marble like stars
snagged on a black river. Brass candelabra glowed in
rows, the beeswax pillars already leaning with melt, their
perfumed smoke braided with frankincense. Incense
crawled up the vaulting ribs and pooled beneath the rose
window like a weather system. Every step sounded
ceremonial whether anyone intended it or not; even
breath felt like part of a rite.

They had remade the sanctuary into a war-room.
On the altar, vestments lay in cardinal red and host-
white, draped with a care that bordered on tenderness. A
silver reliquary the size of a child's forearm gleamed with
its guarded splinter, lignum crucis, the old label read,
spidery Latin hand. A chalice that had burned twice and
survived thrice sat heavy, the gold dimmed by time in a
way that made it more dangerous, not less. A
monstrance flared on its stand, a burst of rays that
caught and broke candlelight into thin knives. Beside the
pulpit, swaddled in linen like a relic of its own, the
Folium Obscurum, the blood-written page, rested inside
a glass case whose lid was latched but not locked. They
had agreed on that: nothing that came next could be
done with locked things.

At the center of the sanctuary, where the worn steps
met the marble sea, a chair awaited: thick oak, iron-
banded, the restraints bolted to its arms and legs broad
enough for wrists that might tear tendons to slip free. It
was ghastly and necessary.

Father Michael walked the nave in slow procession
though no bell rang, the collar against his throat a little
too tight, like a hand that hadn't yet squeezed. The stone
remembered weddings he'd blessed, a dozen funerals he
had stumbled through without crying, one baptism
where a baby kicked a shoe off and squealed so loudly a
photographer turned the flash off out of pure reverence

for lungs that strong. He forced his mind to hold those ordinary sacraments. He needed to stand inside them. The oily shadow that clung to the air, another smell under the incense, not rot exactly, more like a cellar that had never seen light, kept trying to coax his mind toward the hurricane night, the drowned knocking, the mud-dark water.

Sister Helena drifted beside him; rosary coiled in her palm like a small serpent asleep. Candle fire brushed her cheekbones; the little lift of chin looked less like defiance than promise not to run.

"Every stone here has absorbed prayer for more than a century," she said, not to cheer him but as a fact. "It will not be a neutral witness."

"I need it to be a wall," he whispered.

"It will be what it can be," she said. "Walls fall. Sometimes they ring instead."

At the side doors, Sean Sullivan carried Ashlyn as if she were a newborn and death both. His face had carved itself into something older in the last weeks, cheeks not so much gaunt as chiseled; mouth pressed in a learned line because if it loosened it would break. Nora walked at his elbow, one hand on Ashlyn's bare foot, as if the contact could ferry warmth along a wire. Bishop Shaw had promised discretion, and the guards outside had turned eyes blank as marble, heads bowed. Inside, the Sullivans moved through candle-scent like sailors coming up in fog to a coast they had been told was there.

They laid Ashlyn into the heavy chair. Nora smoothed her hair back, gently, the way mother's smooth hair only when a child sleeps or is hurt. The straps closed with careful clicks, not the violent tug of a cop car's door but the final snug of a harness a climber trusts. Father Michael watched the muscles in Sean's jaw jump as the last buckles tightened.

Ashlyn looked out at them with a stillness that was wrong. Over the past month, her body had learned to thrash with monstrous strength; her voice had convulsed. This calm felt worse. The eyes were bottomless pits lacquered to the mirror-sheen of wet obsidian. A cracked smile touched the mouth as if it had remembered a picture of a child smiling and was trying to arrange muscle to match.

"Hi, Daddy," she said in her own voice. The word shaved Sean thin.

Nora kissed her on the forehead.

"We're here."

Ashlyn turned her head slightly toward the altar. The pupils didn't dilate; they widened like holes widening.

"Fiat lux," she whispered. "Et lux facta est."

Her voice shifted on the last word, layering, harmonics blooming through the nave the way a pipe organ swell. The line from Genesis should have carried creation in it; here it carried imitation.

"And the Pope wept when I spoke through the child," the voice added conversationally, as if reminding old friends of a charming anecdote. It was the Folium's line, the one that had made Kearns go quiet when he read it.

Candleflames went thin, blue-tipped, as if what had spoken was oxygen.

Father Michael took one step closer to the chair and felt, like a hand brushed across his scalp, the thrill that comes before a lightning strike. He forced the breath to go all the way down.

"We're beginning," he said, to the team, to the thing. "Now."

Procession and Placing

They moved like a small liturgy. Sister Helena took the lead, head dipped for a heartbeat, and then raised, and then dipped again, less bow than a steadying nod to the Invisible. Daniel Kearns. Collar starched, eyes older than his age, brought the Gospel book up the steps, hands firm. Behind him, Dr. Elias Kearns carried a brass ewer as if it were breakable thought; the water inside sloshed and ringed the rim with a bright wet line. Sean and Nora followed their daughter's chair, each with one

hand on the wood as if shouldering a casket. Father
Michael walked last, the crucifix pressed to his chest
until the wood's corners left little bruises he wouldn't
feel until tomorrow.

At the altar rail, they fanned to posts they had
agreed on in whispers over the last hours. Sister Helena
by the girl's left shoulder, rosary and ritual layered in her
memory like two cloths overlaying the same table.
Father Michael directly in front, the place where ridicule
would land first. Daniel at the right shoulder to read, to
bless, to argue with doubt out loud. Elias, pale, jaw
clenched, by the pulpit, near enough to the Folium to
open it if necessity demanded, far enough that his hands
might not shake into mistake.

"Adjúro te," Sister Helena said, not the rite yet, just
the verb and its target: I adjure you. She didn't call the
name. They had decided: the name was dynamite, not
incense.

Ashlyn blinked slowly, lids coming down too far
and rising back not quite to where lids are supposed to
rest.

"Adjúro te," she echoed pleasantly, and then, with
the warmth of an old teacher greeting a pupil, "Start
with the opening. I love when you start with the
opening."

Sister Helena flicked her eyes at Father Michael. Are
you steady?

His hand tightened on the crucifix. He used the pain.

"We begin," he said, to the girl, to the heaven that watched, to himself.

He nodded, and Sister Helena drew a breath as if plunging.

The Opening Litany

"Adjúro te, omnis immundíssime spíritus, omnis Satanáica potéstas, omnis incúrsio adversárii, omnis légio, omnis congregátio et secta diáboli…*"

Her Latin came out like silver wire, fine but tensile. The long sentence braided categories of enemy with an old precision that had felt archaic in seminary and now felt like listing floodgates on a dam: every bolt named so none could slip.

"…ergo, draco maledícte, et omnis légio diáboli…"

Ashlyn's lips moved one beat ahead. Not repeating so much as conducting, tossing back each clause a fraction sooner, parodying cadence. Her eyes didn't track Sister Helena's mouth. They tracked the crucifix the way a cat tracks a fly.

Daniel began a counterpoint, Kyrie eleison rising and falling under the Latin as if the nave had a second heartbeat. He scattered holy water in arcs that crossed and crossed again; the droplets caught light and became briefly beaded crowns where they landed on Ashlyn's skin before evaporating at contact. This was new. In the house, the water had hissed; here it vanished like breath on glass.

"Exorcízo te, immundíssime spíritus," Sister Helena pressed, heat in the words. "In nómine Dómini nostri Iesu Christi…"

The girl shifted in the chair, straps creaking. Her smile spread. When she answered this time, the voice went deeper, a resonant chant, the diction clipped and formal.

"Summis desiderantes affectibus," it intoned.

"You call me devil; your Pope called my servants witches."

Kearns flinched. The old bull of Innocent VIII had been the scholar's first brush with church power and silence.

"It's quoting the decree," he said hoarsely. "Word for word."

"Summis desiderantes," the voice purred again, now higher. "Quae non obstantibus, oh, forgive my Latin, Father Donnelly. It's better than yours."

Father Michael bit the inside of his cheek until he tasted iron. He had learned to read Canon Law like an honest man reads a manual, carefully, with more faith in paper than himself. Hearing the voice throw the law back like a joke cut deeper than he wanted to admit.

He lifted the crucifix.

"You will leave." He kept it short, English flat, because anything longer would risk echo.

Ashlyn cocked her head. The room brightened by a hair, no, the candleflames thinned, the way flames do when they're about to go blue.

"Will," she repeated in English, each consonant a click. "Voluntas. Your mother had one too."

The hurricane noise rose in his skull, the wooden slats of the confessional swelling, the knocking not panicked but measured, knock…knock…knock, as if the one inside had learned that measured might make a priest come. Father Michael's stomach flipped; his foot shifted back on marble he had mopped as a young curate. He measured his breath in fours. He did not look at the box down the side aisle.

Sister Helena shot him a side glance that said both stay and hear only me.

"Ergo, draco maledícte…"

The girl sighed theatrically.

"Do you tire your tongue, sister? Do you tire it like you tired it in Oaxaca?" The voice lightened, taking on a woman's cadence, the mother who'd thanked Sister Helena for the miracle.

"Gracias, hermana." Then it slid into the father's voice, bruised with grief that had not yet turned to rage:

"Qué hiciste? What did you bring to my son?"

Sister Helena's hand stuttered on a bead. The rosary twanged, a tiny sound in that vast air, but Daniel's head snapped toward it as if someone had fired a gun.

"Stay," Father Michael whispered, this time to her.

She nodded once, tightened the coil until her fingers blanched, and drove on: "Imperat tibi Deus Pater, imperat tibi Deus Filius, imperat tibi Deus Spiritus Sanctus…"

The chair thunked; the straps tugged; wood protested with a long, fibrous noise. Ashlyn's body arched a fraction, muscles asserting the physics of terror, but the mouth laughed.

"Three names," it said gently. "Three Persons. Three failed nights, if you keep this pace."

Candles three pews back went out in a chain, pff pff pff, and the darkness behind Father Michael felt like a set of hands that had not yet decided where to touch.

Scripture Mocked

The Gospel book gleamed in Daniel's hands. He opened, not to assigned reading but to the place his fingers found as if the leather knew: John 8, the light passage he'd read to freshmen who mistook exegesis for debate.

"Ego sum lux mundi," he read, voice steady, and even reading the Latin he released the English the way a teacher releases chalk, efficient, unadorned. "He who follows Me shall not walk in darkness, but shall have the light of life."

"Oh, yes," the voice crooned. "Light. What a useful word. Did you ever notice," it confided to Father Michael, "that no one ever says shadow without first teaching it light?"

Then the tone changed. Deepened. Carried a cadence that pricked Kearns' ears with the memory of televised midnight Masses, the solemn swell of a pontiff's Latin delivered to silent tens of thousands.

"Quo primum tempore…" the voice began, naming a decree far from its proper subject and dragging it into this present as if to say every paper is mine. "…missae celebrandae ritum… Oh, child," it said to Nora, kindly, 'the Mass rite for celebration.' "I have celebrated so many rites in so many mouths."

Nora made an animal sound and bent forward over her folded hands. Under the pew, her heel slid on wax and she steadied herself on the wood with a little gasp, embarrassed at noise at the wrong time like it was still Mass and she'd dropped a hymnal.

Kearns' voice burst out too loud in the hush.

"Stop, stop grafting authority you despise!" The scholar was there again, the one who barked at grad students when they fumbled a date by a century.

"You don't own these texts."

The girl turned the head slowly toward him; the smile went smaller and more precise.

"You don't either," she said sweetly. "But you fed on them so hungrily you forgot your son's face."

Daniel flinched, and then flinched from the flinch, furious with himself for letting his father matter. He crossed himself so hard his fingers clicked against his forehead, his chest.

"In the name of the Father," he said, English now, not to be echoed, "and of the Son, and of the Holy Spirit"

"Son," the voice purred, and the word elongated into a noose.

"Hijo. Would you like to see him? Tu niñez. The boy at nine in his altar server cassock? The boy at twelve who found a book under your father's bed and read till dawn and wondered why it lied better than prayer? The boy at sixteen who stood in a doorway and watched his mother cry into a sink?"

"Enough!" Sister Helena snapped, not at Daniel but at the air, and the snap cut cleanly because it was the first time her voice had thrown no liturgy at the shadow at all. The shadow licked it like cream.

"Enough?" it repeated delightedly. "We have only begun. We haven't even touched water yet."

Assault of the Past

It came like weather, so fast there was no warning and yet if you watched film back you could say the clouds had thickened five minutes before.

Father Michael's knees gave, he didn't intend to kneel, he didn't choose humility. He simply wasn't standing anymore. The smell arrived first: wet wood, damp coats hung in a vestibule, the copper penny-bite of a body that has panicked in water and voided without meaning to. The confessional box in the east transept did not move, but in his periphery, it was evening-dark the way things get in churches even at noon because stained glass is a kind of night. The knock came inside his sternum, three thuds timed to the rhythm of his heart's diastole.

"Father?" The voice was small. The age was wrong. He had never heard the addict's voice as anything but rough-throated, middle-aged, but voices in dreams borrow mouths.

"Father, I don't want to die in it."

His breath chopped. He pictured the addict's hands gripping the wooden grill, gone white at the knuckles, that useless reflex we have to hang on to objects when drowning in air. He pictured the water creeping under the door like a dog nosing a threshold. He tasted his mother's hospital room, which made no sense, linoleum

190

and hand sanitizer and the faint sweetness of morphine, inside the same breath. The two rooms overlapped in his head in a map where streets had the same name.

Sister Helena swayed. Oaxaca came not as a room but as a heat, a sweat-slick drip down every vertebrae as if someone had poured a small stream under the skin. The boy's spine had bent in her memory like a sapling under a burden of fruit; his mouth had filled with foam that wasn't, and when she pressed a cloth, it came away dotted with pink. The mother had kissed the nun's hands after the false morning, kissed hard, pressed the lips as if to draw the bone to tongue so that the blessing could be ingested.

"Milagro." And three days later that mouth had spat curses until the voice broke, not because Spanish lacked words but because the throat tore.

Kearns went down against the marble with a thump that rang. He saw Daniel at eight, heels banging the pew because eight-year-old legs don't reach the floor. The boy's face was upturned toward the priest lifting the host and the boy's eyes were huge because he had learned in school that it was a miracle, not metaphor, miracle, and nobody had told him yet that fathers can make metaphors out of miracles and fillet them like fish. Kearns heard himself twenty years younger, saying to a colleague, The safer the Church sounds, the more it's hiding, and he wanted to go back in time and slap his own mouth shut.

Daniel, for his part, saw himself at sixteen in the hallway, watching his father not look up from a stack of photocopies as his mother pressed a hand to her eye for longer than a hand to an eye needs to be pressed; he saw himself at nineteen, telling a spiritual director that he wanted to be a priest because somebody had to love God in this family, and the director had said softly, Is that love or a wager? and he had said, Does it matter?

Nora rose half out of the pew, ready to run not toward her daughter but toward the team to pull them up like she'd pull strangers off a train track, the old mother-trope, save the ones saving her child. Sean wrapped a hand around her wrist and anchored both of them back to kneel because he knew if they started walking now, they'd walk forever.

Ashlyn's body vibrated in the restraints like a string drawn too tight. The mouth opened and the three voices talked at once like a chorus each singing a different verse and somehow you could understand all the words:

"You left me in the water."

"You made me dance to your prayer and then you broke my bones."

"You chose paper. You chose a different altar."

Daniel shouted over them, "Lord Jesus Christ, Son of the living God"

"Have mercy," the voices chimed, and then laughed, not at the mercy but at the timbre, like they'd nailed the impression.

The rafters above the nave creaked in a way that was physics, not haunting, a building speaking under strain. Something feather-light sifted down, a dusting of plaster that smelled faintly of lath, old horsehair. Under it the incense swam and then steadied.

"Now," Sister Helena breathed, eyes wide and steady as a sniper.

Father Michael pushed up, palms sliding a fraction on marble slick with holy water. The crucifix seared his skin, and he chose to believe the burn wasn't mockery. He lifted it and did not announce in Latin because he had learned the last weeks that Latin could become a stage too big for him to stand on. He spoke like a man into another man's face:

"You will not have her. In the name of Christ, you will not."

"Name," the demon sighed, like a gourmand complaining of a dish grown dull.

"You stand in a house of names. Call me something and I will try it on and parade in it."

Sister Helena cut across with a shard of psalm "Dominus lux mea et salus mea"

"quem timebo?" the voices sang back in the round.

"Whom shall, I fear? Oh, how I adore your rhetorical questions."

Fire in the Mouth

Daniel lifted the aspergillum; water filmed the air in glitter and vanished on contact with Ashlyn's skin like drops hitting a griddle. Steam rose faintly, enough to be seen by the eye, not enough for cameras to catch if cameras were allowed.

"Again," Sister Helena said.

Daniel's jaw set. He dipped, flung; dipped, flung. The rhythm steadied him. The water became rosary beads thrown, each one a little Hail Mary bead skipping across a black lake and sinking without a sound.

Kearns moved with the stiffness of a man accused by a voice only he could hear, and set the ewer down, and picked up the Gospel like a shield. He read through a throat gone raw, not because he trusted the reading but because he knew the sentence: the light shines in darkness and the darkness did not comprehend it. The Greek came to mind before the Latin κατέλαβεν to seize, to overcome, to grasp. The scholar mind said, pedantic and kind, it can mean not understood as much as not overpowered. The other part of him said, God, I never understood anything, and the two parts collided and made a third: Try anyway.

"Et verbum caro factum est," he read, and the thing in Ashlyn went still for a single blink as if the Incarnation had registered as a word that tasted like metal on the tongue. Then the smile returned, wider.

"Caro," it crooned. "Flesh." The tongues of the three voices slid hard on the r. "Do you know what bodies do in water, Father Donnelly? Do you know how long the lungs fight after the knock stops?"

Father Michael didn't move. He breathed four in, four held, four out, four held, a square for a square of marble.

Sister Helena stepped closer, crucifix poised, forehead shining with sweat.

"Umbra Dei," she said, not shouting, not dramatic, just the way a person would say a liar's name on a witness stand, making a record. "You are named."

The candles leapt. The shadow under the chair thickened as if the light itself had mass and was pooling elsewhere.

Something cracked high up, a small noise, real, a hairline flare in a lancet window where lead had grown brittle. A second later, a flake of blue glass fell and shattered on the marble like a toy bell. Daniel flinched. The monstrance didn't move.

Ashlyn's lips peeled back; teeth showed, child's teeth edged in the grime of too many days not being brushed because whose hand could persuade those lips

195

to part and not get bitten. Smoke curled from her mouth, thin as incense.

"Ascensio est mea," she breathed, and rose in the chair, not the body alone now but the whole wood, the iron, lifted three inches, then six, then a foot, straps alive when they should have been still. The bolts whined; the floor left the chair behind; and up at the organ loft a wind that had not been asked for went through the pipes and made a single note that sounded like a human throat discovering it had room to scream.

Sean half rose and Nora dragged him back with both hands.

"Don't," she hissed, not at the devil but at her husband, because one man grabbed by the air in front of a child is better than two.

"Now," Sister Helena said, not because she thought the moment was right in any mystical sense but because you choose moments or moments choose you.

Father Michael pressed the crucifix to the girl's brow. The metal hissed. A streak of angry red rose under it like a brand.

"You are unseated," he said, English, blunt. "You are named and unseated."

The three voices wove themselves into a braid of sound that somehow held words: "Name me and I come closer. Touch me and I burn you. Pray me and I repeat you. Bleed, priest. Bleed."

"Don't," Sister Helena snapped, knowing exactly what his hand wanted: to reopen the cut and give blood because the Folium had promised that blood spoke a language shadow could not echo.

"Not yet. Not on its cue."

His hand trembled. He did not cut. He held. He pressed. He swallowed the bile that rose at the memory of the house, how easily the shadow had caught his words and thrown them back like darts.

The chair sagged back to the floor with a thud that reverberated up his tibias. The straps tightened of their own accord, leather squealing through buckles, and when they lay flat again the buckles were hooked. Father Michael saw no hands. He felt no wind.

Ashlyn breathed out like a runner after a sprint. The breath made the candleflames dip along the first row like a wave. She smiled.

"Again."

Sister Helena Falters

The ritual crawled forward in pulses, heat and slack, laughter and grit, until time took on the queer elasticity pain gives it. At some point, Sister Helena felt the building tilt, not physically but in meaning: a church is a container for prayer, but when prayer is mocked inside it, the mind has to decide whether the mockery or the prayer defines the space. She knew better than most that the mind's decision can make the floor stay firm. She had learned that in Rome on nights when shrieks bounced off frescoes and old statues watched with blank eyes, and the young priest beside her had whispered that his tongue felt glued to his teeth.

Another gust in her own head brought Oaxaca back, a detail she had not remembered in years. The boy had a scar in the shape of a crescent by his left ear, a scythe of healed flesh from a fall when he was three. Why that detail now? She didn't know, except that guilt is not only the great general; it's also a quartermaster who keeps an inventory with a fetish for minutiae.

"I burn still," the voice said through Ashlyn's mouth in the exact timbre of the old woman whose diary Sister Helena had translated, the martyr who had begged not to be prayed for because prayer had become a lever the shadow could lean on.

Sister Helena's world went white around the edges. She was back at the little desk in the convent archive in Rome, lamp lit, moths beating against the window and then going dead still as the night cooled. She had whispered the line to herself because she wanted the Latin to feel like hers in her mouth before she put it on paper.

She had said it softly, "Ardeo adhuc," and the hairs on her arms had risen, and she had told herself it was because she loved language.

"Look at me," Father Michael said, low and sharp.

Her eyes snapped to his. He didn't give her comfort. He gave her a job.

"Say the psalm," he said.

"Which psalm?" She opened her mouth and the right one came as if her ribs had memorized the rhythm:

"Quia tu, Domine, spes mea"

The voice beat her to the next words.

"Altissimum posuisti refugium tuum."

"Keep going," Father Michael said, and she did, and the shadow repeated like a child anticipating the punchline of a joke it's heard a hundred times and loves because it knows it.

Beads rolled underfoot, three of them had snapped free earlier; now they found the little dips in marble worn by a hundred years of shoes and came to rest against the chair leg like spent rounds.

"Sister Helena," the voice breathed, switching to Spanish so quick anyone not from there would think the language itself had exorcised the Latin.

"No fue milagro." Not a miracle.

"Fue invitación." An invitation.

She flinched and then set her jaw.

"Then hear this," she said in English. "You are unwelcome." She didn't say I unwelcome you, because the I gave the shadow a hook. She put the sentence on the air like a sign posted on a door: by order, not plea.

A hairline crack webbed away from the place where the blue shard had fallen. The cathedral made a tired groan the way old timber does when it remembers storms. Under everything, the organ's single held note thinned and died.

Shredding the Priest

The demon turned to Father Michael in full. Maybe it had been playing him like a background instrument, knock, knock; drown, drown, and had decided the melody needed a solo.

"Law school dropout," it said lightly, like a friend teasing. "Mama's boy. Collar borrower. Professional comforter." Each phrase came in a different voice: a snide one, a fond one, one like an administrative assistant who had learned to wield politeness as a blade.

Father Michael almost laughed, some part of the mind sometimes tries to survive by framing a pattern as ridiculous, but the laugh lodged because of the timing: the last line matched exactly a parishioner's tone the year of the hurricane.

"You are so good at talking to people, Father" the week before he had not opened the box.

He lifted the crucifix higher. The heat in the wood had cooled; now it felt like weight, honest, not mystical.

"You are not the judge here," he said. "You're the thief. Thieves mock the judge and leave in chains." It sounded better in his head than it came out; out loud it sounded like the homily of a man whose analogies work until something living steps up to them and breathes.

"You left me in the water," the voice breathed intimately, and his hand shook, but he didn't lower it.

"Say it again," Sister Helena said, low, this time to him, not to the thing.

"Own it and don't let it own you."

"I left him," he said. Not a priest trying to make a point. A man naming his act. "I left him, and I have repented every day."

The voice purred, "And that saves you how?"

"It doesn't save me," he said. "He does." He angled the crucifix, human wood, stubborn symbol, up one inch, enough to make a gesture feel like a stance.

"Christus vincit." He didn't add the rest; he didn't need to risk echo. The three syllables hung.

For the first time since they began, Ashlyn's eyes flicked, not to the crucifix but to the monstrance. The pupils clenched. The mouth twitched. It was minuscule, a micro-expression a jury would miss, and it gave Father

Michael a ridiculous flood of courage that disgusted him even as he took it: you needed a twitch to believe. He took it anyway.

"Daniel," he said, without taking his eyes off the girl, "the Litany of Saints."

Daniel began, not the full chant, which would last an hour, but a rapid bead-string of names said like a list of emergency contacts: "St. Father Michael. St. Raphael. St. Gabriel. St. Peter and Paul. St. Athanasius. St. Teresa of Ávila. St. Catherine of Siena. St. Augustine. St. Monica. St. Patrick." He wanted to stop there, Patrick, the bracelet on Father Michael's wrist burning in cheap metal, but he kept going: "St. Charbel. St. Dymphna. All holy men and women of God."

The shadow laughed at some names (Athanasius made it purr homoousios; Teresa made it sigh oh yes, ecstasy; Patrick made it whisper snakes love islands). At others it fell quiet for a beat no one could time. When Daniel said Monica, Nora sobbed without knowing why. When he said Dymphna, Ashlyn's head gave a tiny jerk like a puppet whose string had been caught on a nail.

"Again," Sister Helena said.

Daniel breathed and did it faster, as if speed could outrun echo. Father Michael thought, fleetingly, stupidly, of baseball announcers listing stats to ward off nerves.

The voices tried to keep up and stumbled on one.

"Char" They smoothed it. "Sharbel." They had mispronounced a saint, and the tiniest sliver of glee pierced Father Michael's chest like sunlight through attic dust.

"Don't gloat," Sister Helena said out of the side of her mouth. "Even in your head."

He didn't smile. He tightened the crucifix grip until the corners bit.

Acceleration

Time changed gears. The demon raked every failure up in handfuls and threw them like ashes in their faces. It dragged out the papal decrees like a litigator slamming binders on a table. It recited Scripture with a music that made beauty itself feel suspect. It squealed in a child register that made Nora's hands flatten on the pew as if to pin herself to wood and not fly apart. It rumbled in a sub-bass that made Sean's teeth feel loose.

The air pressure shifted hard and then let go, shifted and let go, like a cabin losing altitude. The candles did their stubborn work; every time a flame dropped it guttered back, fed by little rivers of wax that made eerie stalactites down the brass. The incense swung a millimeter on its chain and then steadied.

At one surge, the starburst window at the far end moaned, a sound no one could have described later except as stone remembering winter. A hairline crack, thin as the white of an old fingernail, traced itself across a blue pane and stopped.

At another surge, the chair levitated again, an inch this time, and every leather strap thrummed like a plucked string. Father Michael felt something pass by his face, no breeze, more like air displaced by a creature's mass, and smelled a breath that was not rot so much as stale sanctity, the way vestments smell when pulled from trunks un-aired for a century. The thought made his skin crawl: that the thing loved sacred smells because it could wear them and trick the nose.

"Blood," the voice coaxed. "Show me the blood."

"No," Sister Helena said. Then, eight heartbeats later, like a commander pivoting when the board changes:

"Yes, but not as you dictate." She looked at Father Michael and made a tiny cutting motion across her palm.

"Once. On your terms.

He hesitated, the knife a familiar weight, the scar from the house still tender. He drew it across the old line, quick, not a gash, a declaration. Blood bubbled, warm in the cool air. He lifted his hand so his palm hovered over Ashlyn's crown and let a single drop fall.

It struck her hair and didn't vanish. It beaded, ruby under candlelight. A smell rose, hot penny, alive, and the voices gasped together, then laughed, triumph or mockery he couldn't tell, and then coughed, a sound like a singer whose throat has finally found a note it did not like.

"Again," Sister Helena said. "Not more. Again. Words with it."

Father Michael squeezed another drop and spoke not a line from the book but a sentence he had written tears around months ago and never shown anyone:

"I believe You hear me even when I do not hear You."

The drop fell. The laughter stuttered. The chair shook. Ashlyn's eyes flickered, black thinning at the edges, brown trying to make shoreline, and then the voice bulldozed forward, loud to cover the moment:

"Non verbis ordinatis"

Kearns shouted over it, crazier than he had ever sounded in any academic panel, "No ordered words! That's our line!"

The shadow smiled with the girl's mouth.

"And now mine."

Breaking Point

The assault crested. That was the only way any of them could describe it later: not a rock thrown, not a lunge, but a cresting, as if an invisible wave had gathered height behind them for a full hour and now spilled its whole cold face across the sanctuary.

Ashlyn's back bowed so far, the straps groaned. Her jaw unhinged, not horror-movie gape but anatomically wrong in a way that made the eyes water to see. Every candle went horizontal flame for a breath, as if a huge lung had drawn air sideways. The organ moaned again, three notes this time, a chord ghosts might practice.

The voices spoke as one, the child, the man, the abyss, so perfectly braided the ear couldn't separate them anymore: "I am your silence; I am your wound; I am the shadow of your God."

The monstrous part wasn't the content. It was the voice's quiet. It didn't shout that last sentence. It laid it on the marble like a calling card, and the marble did not throw it back.

Father Michael lifted the crucifix, and for the first time, his hand didn't shake.

"No," he said softly. "You are a liar."

"Am I?" The girl's head tilted. "Then prove it."

"Tomorrow," Sister Helena said. She didn't mean to say it aloud. It fell out of her throat anyway, like strategy and prophecy both.

The chair dropped. The straps settled. The candleflames rose and steadied. The organ's breath died.

Ashlyn sat serenely, cheeks slack, the little cracked smile back in place, as if they had wheeled her in and buckled her only five seconds ago and this had been rehearsal. Her eyes were bottomless again.

"This was only the beginning," she said pleasantly, and her gaze slid past Father Michael to the monstrance for the briefest blink, and then back.

No glass fell. No stone cried. The cathedral held its breath, then released it.

Sean slumped as if a string had been cut and Nora caught him with a practiced hand. Daniel lowered the Gospel until it rested against his thigh, his knuckles splotched red where nails had bitten palm. Kearns leaned both hands on the pulpit and bowed his head like a man not praying, just too tired to keep it up.

Father Michael drew a breath and another, each one a small theft back from the night. He didn't know if they had won or lost or just survived. He knew only that his knees worked and he didn't want to leave the crucifix on the floor ever again.

Sister Helena reached for her rosary, re-coiled it, and looked down at the beads left under the chair, the three that had rolled and come to rest. She let them stay. Not everything broken needs to be fixed this minute.

Above them, the rose window held. The crack in the blue pane made a hair-thin vein through sky. Dawn would come through it differently if it came while they still stood.

"Again," the shadow had said.

"Tomorrow," Sister Helena had answered.

The first assault had ended. The stone remembered them, and the shadow, and all their small, defiant words, and in the cathedral's hush, somewhere high up where the ribs met, the air trembled with a silence so taut it was almost sound, the string between faith and fear pulled to its singing point, waiting to be plucked again.

Chapter 21
The Long Night

"Fides ardens claudit eum; fides fracta aperit januam."
Burning faith binds him; broken faith opens the door.
— *Liber Obscura, Fragmentum 203*

The cathedral didn't empty so much as exhale in ragged drafts, as if the building itself had lungs and they were smoke-sick. The last of the parish guards closed the street doors and the outside world compressed into a ribbon of muffled city-noise, tires hissing, a lone siren veering off somewhere toward the highway, laughter falling in tatters at the edge of Washington Street.

Inside, the candles kept their vigil. Hundreds of beeswax pillars swayed in their brass forests, each flame a little human spine that refused to bow. The incense hung lower now, dulled to a sweet damp tinge like a robe that's been worn too long at wake after wake. On the sanctuary steps, the holy water pooled in a shallow sheen, making the marble look ice-slick; every footfall had to consider balance before belief.

Ashlyn sat in the chair, her lashes lowered like a child sleep-drunk during a long sermon, her mouth fixed at that not-smile. If you didn't know, you could mistake the posture for peace. Everyone here knew. Peace breathes differently.

Nora's knees creaked when she stood. She had been kneeling so long that the stars at the edges of her sight had arranged themselves into rosary decades. Sean hadn't stood at all. He crouched in a way no back can forgive, fingers welded around the oak armrest as if he were the one braced to be carried away. He kept his eyes on his daughter's cheek, the place he had kissed a thousand times in smaller years, because any other place on her face might speak back.

"Take her home," Sister Helena said. Not a request. A verdict from a woman who had stood in enough rooms like this to hear when a room had done all it could.

"No more straps tonight. The ground has swallowed enough."

Sean surfaced from whatever fathom he was in, jaw jerking.

"And if" His voice snagged. He swallowed. "If it... finishes this. If I wake up and she's"

"Then she's with you," Father Michael said, and it felt like a sin to speak it and a sacrament to mean it. He hated the chair in that moment with the pure, childish hatred one saves for the thing you can blame that is not the person you love.

Daniel moved to the buckles. He didn't rush. He pressed each tongue free, laid each strap aside with the courtesy one affords a sleeping patient. The leather had warmed to skin and retained that warmth like memory; the smell of it filled the space between his ribs and made him think of his own confirmation day, chrism oil and leather shoes and his father not there.

When the last strap came loose, Ashlyn opened her eyes. Brown. For a heartbeat. For a whole grace-long heartbeat.

"Daddy?" It was raw cotton, that voice, raspy from screaming. A child's quake under it, the little animal fear that lives in every fourteen-year-old who has ever been truly hurt and knows this is no longer a game adults can fix.

Sean folded around her, the way a man folds only when something more important than bone is at risk. He lifted her and the chair groaned at the sudden absence of weight. Ashlyn's arms slid to his neck without muscle, her hands almost weightless, then one finger twitched and pressed into his skin like a punctuation mark.

"I'm tired," she whispered into him.

"I know, baby." He was crying and didn't know it, the tears warm tracks that the night air cooled.

"I'm not," came the other voice, amiable as a guest declining coffee. No one but Sean heard it; he heard it like a flaw in a bell.

Nora rose and laid the rosary in Ashlyn's palm, not forcing the fingers closed, just letting gravity choose if beads would stay. They did. For now.

The nave doors opened, letting the night finger in. The family slipped through the seam where sacred joins ordinary, and the doors kissed shut behind them with the gentleness of someone tucking a child in and not wanting to wake her.

Silence fell like curtain-weight.

Elias Kearns coughed once to reset the theater of his own throat, but the sound came out as a cracked laugh that embarrassed him. He gripped the pulpit like men grip hospital railings when elevators drop that first inch.

"We lost," he said to the wood, to the book, to the crucifix that watched without blinking. "We dressed it like survival, but we lost."

Sister Helena turned, and candlelight made hard planes of her cheeks.

"We did not lose," she said, and her voice made the statement sound like a rock placed where a wall used to be. "We were not devoured. We are standing. That counts. Standing counts."

Father Michael had not moved. The crucifix left four tiny rectangles stamped into his palm, and the pain felt truthful in a way theology sometimes didn't. He

didn't disagree. He didn't agree. He breathed, the oldest
liturgy he knew.

The monstrance threw a thin spear of light across
his hands; it wobbled when the candle nearest it guttered
and steadied when the wick found itself again. That little
wobble rescued him, absurdly. Even holy light shakes
sometimes and then goes right back to shining.

"Go," Bishop Shaw said from the shadows, no
grandeur, no bishop's baritone, just a tired man who had
stood in the back and not noticed his presence into the
story because sometimes Church is wise enough to let
priests and nuns be Church without her. "Sleep. Eat.
Pray if you can. Tomorrow, we name morning by what
we do in it."

No one bowed. No one saluted. They nodded as if
the word had been amen.

Drift

The rectory had the same smell it always had, old
wood, coffee, wax, but tonight it felt like a stage where
last act pieces had been moved out and you could see
scuff marks the set hid. The hallway crucifixes were all
righted now; someone (Father Michael couldn't
remember who) had rehung the one near the kitchen
that used to tilt like a comma.

He went to his room and took the collar off. The
little white tab clicked on the nightstand like a tooth. He
didn't undress. He sat on the bed's edge, the Bible on his
lap because his hands needed something that would not
answer back like a voice does when it is borrowed by a
very old enemy.

The Bible fell as books fall, by habit, to a place that
had been warmed by usage: Tobit. He hated that. He
wanted the Spirit to do the opening if it meant to speak,
not the paper to yield to his own grease. Still, the fish
read him; the ash read him; the promise and the
incompleteness read him. The page seemed to hold
breath like a person does before speaking. It did not
speak.

"Lord," he said, and heard how small he sounded.
"If I am only absence, use the shape of it. Fill it how
You want, but please, please, if You need a man, let me
do."

Silence. Not hostile. Not warm.

He lay back without remembering lying back and
woke four minutes later with the same sentence in his
head, as if his own brain refused to shut down the plea.

Sister Helena did not go to a bedroom. She went to
the sacristy, because her body had learned over decades
that when language collapses, the best place to wait for it
to come back is near linen folded with exactness. She set
her rosary on the wooden surface the way surgeons set

instruments, rows, gleam, order, a choreography that returns the heart to its original tempo.

She did not pray. She breathed. The Our Father would wait under that breath the way a seed waits under frost; the problem tonight was not that she didn't know the words. It was that the words had been mocked to her face, and no warrior likes seeing their weapon paraded around the town square.

Oaxaca lived behind her eyelids. Not the convulsions, not the death. A stupid detail: the boy had a whale on his T-shirt, faded at the tail because he slept on that side and shirts wear out where bodies are softest. Why now? Why this? She almost laughed. The mind is a magpie; it drags bright bits to the nest when storms rise.

She pressed her forehead against the prie-dieu and let the wood leave its shallow cold on her skin.

"I know who You are," she whispered without meaning to. "Even when I don't like what You let happen, I know who You are." That didn't fix anything. It made a floor.

Elias Kearns didn't mean to drink. He had stopped for years, out of spite first (if Rome would not let him be right, he would at least be sober) and then out of pride (he could do it himself). Tonight, pride and spite were cheap paper when rain hits them. The first sip burned. The second didn't. The third made him tilt his head back and press his eyes shut, and behind his lids he saw

Daniel at ten with a book bigger than his chest and a joy so unguarded that Elias had looked away because he didn't know how to love someone who didn't need arguing with.

He went back into the nave alone, he hated himself for it, the theatricality, the scholar in the afterhours looking for a line only he could footnote and stood under the pulpit anyway. The Folium shivered faintly under glass as if the letters in the blood were worms shifting when rain hits dirt. He did not open it. He did not touch the case. He stood and tried to stare it down like a rival across a table.

"Read me, Daddy," a voice said. Not Daniel grown, not Daniel boy, some in-between register memory makes when it wants to break you and pet you both.

He put the flask away. He did not cry. He allowed himself five seconds of thinking he might, and then he didn't. The shadow would love those tears too much.

Daniel walked the aisles and flung cold water like a farmer flings seed when the field is already tilled and storm-dark but you plant anyway because waiting will starve you. He didn't pray with words. His mouth moved; if someone had gotten close, they would have heard numbers. He was counting pews. He made it to fifty-six and then lost his place and said damn too loudly for a cathedral and stopped, ashamed, amused, angry, all layered.

He found himself in the east transept and didn't intend to look at the confessional but did. The wood was just wood. The doors were just doors. The seat inside had the shape of a thousand anxious penitent backsides pressed into it. He opened the door and sat and shut it and listened. He wanted a knock. He wanted to prove to himself that emptiness is what it is when the demon is not invited. The only sound was the click of an old hinge resenting new gravity.

"Forgive me," he said finally, not to a man behind a lattice but to a God who had listened to more stupid sins than Daniel would ever manage.

"For wanting to win more than save. For wanting him", he had to force his mouth to say him, "my father, to see me win."

He expected silence. He got it. It did not feel like rejection this time. It felt like the only answer that would not feed the wrong mouth.

The Family House

On O'Reilly Street, the storm-smell lived in the drywall now. Houses keep things. Nora turned the porch light on and then off and on again as if the light's decision would make the night pick a mood. Inside, she pulled the curtains because curtains make priests and demons both feel like they're not being watched.

She and Sean laid Ashlyn in her bed. They replaced her pillow with a cooler one because mothers do that even when their children are grown and insistent about not being tucked. The sheets had been washed this afternoon in the twenty-minute window when Nora could believe fabric mattered; the lavender softener smelled like the only summer they could afford to take a week in New Hampshire and pretend lakes could fix things.

Ashlyn's eyes fluttered. She turned her head, mouth tilting toward Nora's hand like a plant turns to a window.

"Mom," she said on a sigh.

"I'm here, my love."

"Tell me the story," she whispered, and for a breath Nora thought the one about the fox and the bread and the river, the story her children used to request because Sean could make the fox's voice sound like a man at the pub. She opened her mouth.

"Tell me the story," Ashlyn repeated, and this time the vowels tilled wrong, and the mouth smiled too long after the word ended, and Sean put his hand on Nora's wrist because he heard it too.

"What story?" Nora asked, because sometimes you don't run; you ask questions to keep the room yours.

"The story where I get to stay," the voice said, and then, cheerfully, like a teacher who has flipped a page,

"Tell me the story where I burn."

Nora closed her eyes.

"No."

"Then I'll tell it."

The voice said, pleasant as a kettle about to boil, and Ashlyn's head sank into the pillow and she slept, or wore sleep like a coat that fit too well.

Sean sat guard. He dragged the old chair from the hallway and planted it by the bed and put a baseball bat under it because the human brain was not made to spend a night without an object you can swing. The bat had SULLIVAN burned on it from when Patrick was twelve and Sean had money for that sort of sentimental overkill. He ran his thumb over the letters until the skin warmed.

"Do you remember the day we brought her home?" he asked the dark, and the dark did not answer and that was mercy. Sometimes memory answers too quickly and it's worse.

Nora fell asleep in the doorway in that folded way people sleep when they refuse beds. She slept with her hand on the doorframe as if a door is a person, you can hold upright.

Around two, Ashlyn sat straight up without using her hands. Sean lurched forward, the bat clattering, but she only looked at the wall where her sigils still bled through the paint. In the blueish streetlight that sneaks

through every curtain, the marks looked like a foreign
alphabet that refuses translation. Ashlyn's lips moved.
The syllables were Latin. The tone was nursery rhyme.
She counted backwards from twenty-seven in a melody
the Sullivans didn't know, and when she reached unum
she smiled and lay back down.

The bat felt heavier. Sean didn't put it away.

Morning Triage

Dawn came in grey slices through the sacristy
blinds. The city started itself up: vans beeping, pigeons
bickering, a man on his phone pacing outside and
laughing too loudly at nothing. The cathedral's belly
heard it and did not change shape.

They gathered in the rectory dining room. The table
had a scar across the wood from a Thanksgiving lintel
mishap three pastors ago. Coffee steamed, dark and
hostile, in a pot that had stained its own glass. Someone
had found bread and peanut butter and laid them at the
center like peace offerings to stubborn gods. No one
took any.

Sister Helena placed the Folium Obscurum in the
center and unwrapped it as if unwrapping a wound. The
parchment did its faint shimmer, not showy, not
paranormal-as-television, just a wetness in the letters like

blood refuses complete dryness where it has once been exposed to breath.

Elias sat with a pencil he hadn't sharpened enough. He turned it in his fingers, then clicked the little brass sharpener and rolled the shavings into a neat ribbon because control is an opiate, and he needed the dose. Daniel stood behind him, not sitting because sitting meant settling and he would not let his body accuse him later of comfort.

Father Michael braced his elbows on the table and pressed temple to knuckle. The KIA bracelet slid up his wrist and then back down; Patrick's name pressed a groove into his skin; the groove steadied him.

"Where did we break?" Daniel asked. He was not accusing. He had that voice some young priests learn early, hold-room voice, not performance, not hush. It made people answer.

"On cue," Sister Helena said. "Every time we took a cue. Every time we let it stage the moment." She tapped the cloth-wrapped knife beside Father Michael's hand.

"Even the blood. We used it when we could not bear not to. It laughed."

"It stumbled when Father Michael bled and said his own prayer," Elias said, eyes on the page. "Not a formula. A sentence no book could own."

"Because it cannot rehearse what you live," Sister Helena said. "It cannot echo what is not written down."

Daniel made a face.

"We can't abandon the rite."

"No," Sister Helena agreed. "We build a house with those beams, but the fire that warms the house comes from a hearth we cannot blueprint."

Elias traced a line in the margin with a finger he forced not to tremble. Non repetere verba. Do not repeat the words.

"We've read this a dozen times," he said. "But last night taught us what it means. Not 'don't recite.' It means: don't feed the echo. Speak in a grammar it can't counterfeit."

Father Michael rubbed the heel of his hand over his eyes, gritty with sleep that hadn't arrived.

"So what? We improvise a liturgy?"

"Not improvise," Sister Helena said, and her refusal was gentle. "This is not jazz. It's vow. You will promise what you can deliver. Not what a page tells you to deliver."

Elias flipped to another fragment and turned the book so the others could see the cramped blood-script along the outer edge. Umbra Dei resurget cum Ecclesia ipsa invocat nomen eius. The Church itself will raise him when she calls his name.

Daniel inhaled sharply.

"We keep naming him."

"We do," Elias said softly. "We feed him with our own dread."

"And yet," Sister Helena murmured, "names bind. Scripture is thick with named adversaries cast down. It is not the naming he loves. It is the fear in the mouth that speaks it. Speak a name without fear, and you hand him a chain. Speak it with fear, and you hand him a crown."

Father Michael thought of the single flicker in Ashlyn's eyes toward the monstrance. It had been quick as fin, but it had been there.

"The Presence bothered it," he said. "Not the brass. Not the rays. Him."

Daniel nodded, face easing for the first time since midnight. "Eucharist is the place where He refuses metaphor," he said. "Shadow can't eat what isn't symbol. He can wear symbol. He can't digest Real."

Elias's mouth twitched. "Careful," he said, and it was a joke and not, because father and son had fought this exact argument around an actual dining table a decade ago and here it was again, now a weapon against a common enemy.

"You'll make me believe again out of spite."

"Good," Daniel said, too fast, then swallowed it and tried again, softer. "Good."

Sister Helena pointed to a different note, one half-hidden by a smear that could be age or hand. Cinere et igne claudetur janua. With ash and fire the door shall be closed.

"Fish. Ash. Fire," Father Michael said. "We've carried the fish in story so long we forgot the ash and fire are not metaphor." He looked at his palm; the cut sealed in a thin red seam.

"Blood is the tinder. Faith is the match. The rite is the hearth. Fire is not words."

"Where did we break?" Daniel asked again, stubborn in the way only a man who has given vows can be stubborn. "Aside from everything."

"When it said your sins for you," Sister Helena said quietly.

"That was all of us," Elias said, and didn't look at his son. "It stole posture. That's what it does, but posture can be stolen back."

"How?" Father Michael asked.

Sister Helena tapped the table, a rhythm with the pads of her fingers. "We stand where we failed. We do not avoid the scene of the crime; we import it. You hear the knocking? You open the confessional. You do not run from the box that choked you. Elias, you hear the boy? You name him, not the demon's voice wearing him, but the boy. You bless what you abandoned. Daniel" she looked at the young priest and let the next line come only when he didn't look away "you pray with your father. Not after. During. Where the shadow likes divides, we give it joined hands and make it choke."

Daniel's throat worked.

"And if he…" He didn't finish, but everyone heard fails.

"Then you hold," Sister Helena said.

Nora knocked, soft. She'd slept an hour, maybe, on the couch by the rectory door; you could still see the seam pressed into her cheek from the upholstery. Sean stood behind her holding Ashlyn like a saint carries a relic, all grief, all awe you despise because awe is what you wanted from a pilgrimage, not a hospital. Ashlyn's face, in daylight, looked sixteen and eight and forty at once.

"Today," Nora said. Not a question. "Today."

Father Michael stood. His knees had that strange float people get after surgeries, as if motion would separate bone from tendon. "Today."

"Do we stop if" Sean's voice was broken glass.

"No," Sister Helena said, and it was not anger. It was mercy. Certainty is sometimes kindness.

The Plan

They wrote it on paper first, not because paper compels demons but because people are braver when ink says this is what we will do.

1) Ground:

The Cathedral of the Holy Cross, high altar, monstrance enthroned. Side chapels sealed. Doors bolted. No watchers except guards. No press. No curious faithful. This is not a spectacle; it is surgery.

2) Relics & Matter:

Monstrance exposed; forty-hour devotion condensed to a burning point.

Reliquary of the True Cross placed at the girl's left shoulder; Gospel at her right.

Ash prepared from the palms of last year's Passion Sunday, mingled with a pinch of salt and the ash of the burned edges of a Folium parchment scrap Sister Helena judged safe to consign (a copy of a copy, Rome would scold her; she would accept the censure).

Fire: new charcoal in a brass brazier, blessed; coals to be kindled at the Creed and kept hot.

3) Roles:

Father Father Michael: confessor and anchor. He will not recite every line. He will speak in living words when the echo rises. He will choose when to bleed. He will stand before the confessional at the moment he hears the knock. He will open it. He will say I am here, not I'm sorry. He will absolve the living in front of the dead.

Sister Helena: rite-bearer and tactician. She will pace the ritual, call the saints, and cut the demon off when it tries to own the tempo. She will command silence when noise is weaponized. She will anoint, ash, and cast when the time hits not the clock but the heart.

Daniel: deacon's fire. He will read the Gospel at a volume that makes echo choke. He will lead the Litany not in showy chant but in soldier cadence. He will hold the monstrance in procession at the final pass and not tremble. He will pray with his father aloud, and he will not rush the words to win.

Elias: scholar turned witness. He will not argue. He will stand where his son can feel him at his shoulder and say Amen at the right times. He will open the Folium only when Sister Helena nods. He will close it when she lifts her hand. He will bring the ash bowl at the sign and not spill it. He will name his boy who is not here by his baptismal name and not by the grief-name he uses in his sleep.

4) Parents:

Nora and Sean in the first pew, not as spectators but as participants. Nora to sing a hymn the demon cannot parody because she will change the melody every line; Sean to answer with the same line in his own words. They will not stare at manifestations; they will stare at their daughter, and each time the mouth mocks, they will say "We love you, Ashlyn" in whatever language arrives. The demon cannot steal unscripted love.

5) Blood, Ash, Fire (the Folium triad):

Blood: one drop only, at the psalm Out of the depths I cry to You, with Father Michael's sentence that no one can echo because no one else knows it yet, not even him.

Ash: sign of the cross on the girl's forehead and over the straps, with Sister Helena pronouncing a line none of them had seen in any book: "Dust you are and to truth you shall return." (Truth, not us, the demon hates the swap; lies like to be promised to man, not to truth.)

Fire: brazier carried once around the chair in procession, Daniel first, then Elias, then Father Michael, then Sister Helena, clockwise, then counter, to unwrite circles the shadow sketched.

6) The Name:

Uttered once, not as taunt but as indictment: "Umbra Dei: you are the shadow of what you do not own." No repetition. No relish. Spat like a seed you do not plant.

7) Endgame:

The confessional opened at the final Litany stanza. Father Michael inside. Door cracked. He will not wait for a knock. He will say "Bless me, Father," to teach the shadow that he too is a son, and he will answer himself with the absolution the drowned man never received loud, clean, present tense.

The monstrance raised over Ashlyn's crown. The sentence none of them will rehearse spoken by whoever gets it first. (They did not write that sentence down. They wrote: God will give one of us the line.)

They looked at the page as if it might balk. It didn't. Paper is the only brave thing in a room sometimes, because it doesn't know what it records.

"Eat," Sister Helena said, because planning burns sugar. She pushed the peanut butter toward the boys like a mother who'd vowed not to be mother tonight and failed, and thank God for that.

Nora took a slice and pressed it into Sean's hand and he ate two bites without tasting and then tasted the third and almost wept at how ordinary food tries its darling best to be mercy.

Before Dusk

They didn't disperse to nap or shower. No one wanted to leave the proximity of the plan in case distance made courage evaporate like cheap perfume. They did small chores like people do on the morning of a funeral: polished brass, rolled candles down on a towel to even the bottoms, counted matches, mended a tiny tear in an alb sleeve that had bugged Sister Helena for six months and suddenly could not be tolerated. The mending made her near-tearful with the relief of fixing the one thing she could fix without permission.

Daniel went to the confessional and opened the door and sat and closed it and then opened it again. He looked toward the nave and saw no one and still said aloud, "Bless me, Father," and answered himself with the absolution in the tone he had learned from old pastors who knew that the right cadence heals shame. He felt ridiculous. He felt strong. The contradiction didn't cancel; it made a braid.

Elias took out his phone and typed his son's number and then did not press call. He wrote a text and erased it and wrote another and erased it. He finally wrote: Standing at your shoulder tonight, if you'll have me. He hovered over send. He did not press it. He walked into the nave and found Daniel and stood where his son would stand during the Gospel and slipped the phone away and said, "I'll be here," aloud instead.

Daniel nodded without looking.

"Then be."

Father Michael sat in the front pew where he had sat for funerals, weddings, vigils, and one absurd midnight youth lock-in where someone had pulled the fire alarm and he had laughed so hard he had cried. He looked at the altar and the monstrance and the bowl of ash and the brazier and the chair (emptied, back at the Sullivan house) and felt his chest do that tight thing, like fear is a belt on the inside. He closed his eyes and said one sentence that did not feel like prayer and was: "I would like to be brave without needing to be." The silence after did not change, but it felt thinner, as if sound would have no trouble getting through later.

Sister Helena stood by the pulpit and traced the cracks in the marble with the toe of her shoe, counting. She had counted the floor the way some people count sheep the months she had slept in churches with a different demon breathing down somebody else's throat. She never got past twelve. She never believed in twelve like other people did. She liked eleven and thirteen. She stepped on the thirteenth and said, quietly and with venom, "You are not miracle," to a memory that had made a palace of itself in her head. The word left her mouth like a knife thrown with practiced wrist. The air did not catch it. That was fine. The throw was the point.

Twilight

They reconvened with the Sullivans at the cathedral doors as the sky bruised at the edges and the day cooled its shoulders under the shawl of evening. Boston does twilight in a particular way, streetlamps arriving late to the party, the stone taking color like old photographs, the weather deciding if it intends to be damp all night or give courtesy to the lungs. Tonight, it chose damp. Breath made little ghosts as they spoke.

Ashlyn lay in Sean's arms again, lighter than a bundle of blankets should be. Her skin had that translucent hue apples get under way; her lips were too pale for anyone to pretend color meant health, but her hair smelled like Nora's shampoo and that felt like a victory no cathedral could confer.

"Are we ready?" Nora asked, and the foolishness of the question and the need for it struck the same chord in everyone.

"No," Father Michael said honestly.

"Yes," Sister Helena said, meaning a different thing.

"We will be," Daniel said, and Elias, for once in a life of addenda and quibbles, said only, "Amen."

They stepped inside. The nave accepted them the way the ocean accepts boats, indifferent and strong. The candles were new. The ash bowl sat ready. The brazier waited, coal black in the way only future fire is black.

Sister Helena lifted the linen off the Folium and did not open it. She placed her palm on the cloth as if calming an animal.

"Not yet," she told it, half joke, half order. "You serve us this time."

Father Michael moved to the confessional and let his hand rest on the door. He didn't open it. Not yet. He felt no knock. He listened to his own blood drum in his ears and decided not to shame it for being loud.

Daniel went to the sacristy and brought the monstrance out as if carrying a child to baptism. Elias lit the first coal with the patience of a man who has learned that flame makes the rules and your breath must learn its rhythm.

Nora and Sean took the first pew. Nora leaned toward Ashlyn's ear and hummed, off-key in purpose, an old half-remembered lullaby whose melody she changed each line: no echo would find that song. Sean whispered, in a voice like sand rubbed on callus, "We love you," and then, startled by the sound of himself saying a sentence too soft for a bar, he said it again.

Sister Helena looked at Father Michael.

"When you hear it," she said, and didn't have to say the knock.

"I will open," he said.

"And when it says your mother."

"I will not barter." He touched the crucifix. "I know who she loved."

"And when it calls you El Susurro," Sister Helena said to herself, not to him, and smiled without humor. "I will not answer to childhood."

Elias looked at Daniel.

"Pray with me," he said, not pushing apology into the request like a stain-remover, just the two words, clean.

Daniel clenched his jaw. He nodded. "Now."

They bowed their heads. It was clumsy at first, like two men learning to lift a couch without smashing their hands, then it found the old rhythm the human throat remembers even when ideas go thin: Our Father. The words did not feel stolen tonight. They felt like tools passed from hand to hand in a workshop full of work to do.

The cathedral heard them and gathered itself. Stone does that before storms: tightens, braces, gets ready to remember.

Night pressed its face against the stained glass and made the colors richer. A wind went somewhere high in the rafters and the organ dreamed a single low note to itself, the way old wood hums to ward off cracking.

And in the chair, empty for now, waiting for the straps to resume their grim duty, there was an indentation shaped like the back of a small girl. Even absence leaves a form.

"Again," Sister Helena said, to no one and everyone, the same word the demon had used as taunt and she reclaimed as promise.

"Tonight," Father Michael said.

"Together," Daniel said.

"Amen," said Elias.

Nora kissed her daughter's hair. Sean tightened his grip.

The long night had done its work. It had not granted comfort, but it had carved the plan into bone. When dawn came again at the far end of a second war, the city would not know what its old cathedral had held in its ribs. The candles already knew. The stone already decided to stand.

They waited for the doors to close and the bolts to slide, for the match to strike and the brazier to wake, for the chair to take weight, for the first word and the one after that, unscripted, costly, unrepeatable.

The shadow had asked to hear its name. Tonight, it would hear theirs.

Chapter 22

The Final Assault

"Non omnis angelus est lumen; quidam lumen abscondunt, et umbram portant."
Not every angel is light; some conceal the light, and carry shadow.
— *Liber Obscura, Fragmentum 119*

Boston's night pressed its cheek against the stained glass and left breath there. Outside, the South End coughed and laughed and rattled its keys; inside, the Cathedral of the Holy Cross listened with the patience of rock. Candles already burned along the side-aisles, pillars of beeswax set in ranks like men who had decided, for once, to stand and not run. The nave pooled incense and hush. The floor held a faint sheen where holy water had dried and left rings like evaporated prayers.

Father Michael Donnelly paused in the narthex with his hand on the great door's iron strap. He felt, as he had the first time he came here at seven years old, that stepping into the nave was not walking into a place but entering a story, and that the story knew him. The KIA bracelet bit his wrist. Patrick, it read, the cheap metal warmer than his skin.

Sister Helena Duarte stood under the great crucifix and made of the altar a workbench. She slipped linen like a surgeon sheathing a blade. She placed a small brass bowl of ash and salt to the Gospel's left, the reliquary of the True Cross to its right, the chalice centered and turned a quarter-turn until it faced square, so the stem's nick, scar from some fire two pastors ago, wouldn't catch the lace. The monstrance sat enthroned on the corporal, its gilt rays catching candlelight and throwing it back in little knives.

Daniel Kearns tightened the chair's straps with the unshowy competence you'd want in a firefighter or a medic. Leather creaked, a living sound that made Nora flinch even in imagination. Daniel whispered psalms under his breath, not to calm the room but to keep his hands inside himself.

Elias hovered near the pulpit where the Folium Obscurum lay wrapped in linen like a corpse that must not be buried. He did not touch it. He did not trust himself to.

The doors opened, no whisper, no drama, just the honest hinge-noise of wood that had been alive once and remembered. Sean Sullivan came forward carrying his daughter in his arms like a man who will carry something even if it breaks his back. Ashlyn's head rested in the crook of his elbow. Her hair tickled his forearm. Her sneakers were unlaced.

Nora kept pace beside him, a Hail Mary snagging on every step.

"Here," Sister Helena said, and there was something in the small word, finality, mercy, fatigue, the grit of a promise that has gone from idea to vow.

They eased Ashlyn into the oak chair. For a blink of a kind heartbeat, her lashes fluttered and brown eyes showed through, full of human hurt.

"Daddy?" she whispered.

"I'm here," Sean said, and his voice cracked as if it had run into a hole mid-sentence.

Then the mouth smiled, too long, too carefully, and the brown drowned in lacquered black. The straps slid across soft skin and found their buckles with a skilled sound, like the closing of instrument cases before a performance.

"Round two," said three voices with one mouth.

The doors boomed shut behind them like a vault closing over treasure or bones. Candleflames thinned to blue-tipped needles. The cathedral took its breath and held it.

Setting the Theater of War

Sister Helena moved first because somebody had to. She lit a coal in the brass brazier; the coal took flame like a man takes an insult, slowly at first, then thoroughly, then too much. She pinched incense and let it fall. The smoke rose in a white rope, kinked once near the bowl, then climbed true.

Daniel tested the aspergillum. Water flung; beads spattered the marble and left temporary constellations that would fade before anyone could give them names.

Elias unwrapped the Folium enough to slide it under the glass case he had borrowed from the sacristy cabinet, a reliquary turned reading stand. Linen still covered it; he felt the pulse of ink through cloth. Ridiculous, yes. Real, also yes.

Father Michael went to the confessional and put his palm flat against the door he had not opened the night a hurricane punched water sideways through Boston. The wood was cool, as it always is when a hand wants heat.

"Not tonight," he told it, and the grain did not reply, kindness, that silence.

He returned to the sanctuary and took his place before the chair. The crucifix was not hot yet. It would be.

"Ready?" Sister Helena said, not to ask, but to make each of them say yes once.

"Ready," Father Michael said.

"Ready," Daniel said.

"As I'll ever be," Elias managed.

Sean did not answer. He touched Ashlyn's temple with a forefinger and then stepped to the pew with

Nora, where they knelt the way people do when kneeling is the last work, they can do that does not shatter them.

The Opening: Chorus and Counter-chorus

"Adjúro te, omnis immundíssime spíritus," Sister Helena began, and the Latin laid track down the air as surely as streetcar rails are laid in iron. "...omnis incúrsio adversárii, omnis légio, omnis congregátio et secta diáboli."

Echo answered a breath ahead: "Adjúro te... omnis secta..." The cadence was correct. The pronunciation was perfect. The rhythm was one hair wrong, too gleeful, too sure, like a choirboy smirking behind a veil.

Daniel's aspergillum cut arcs and fell into rhythm with Sister Helena's clauses: a score written for water and word. Each drop that touched Ashlyn's forearm hissed like rain on summer pavement. Steam curled sweet as a lie.

Elias's scholar-brain took notes against its will: echo as tactic, exactitude as mockery, the way her mouth formed the u in immundíssime. He wanted to throw the book at the floor and have it break. He wanted to open it and read until dawn. He held both wantings so tightly his hands shook.

Father Michael lifted the crucifix.

"In the name of Christ, leave her."

Ashlyn tipped her head, as if examining an interesting insect on his collar.

"Which name?" three voices asked gently.

"The one you mouth when you feel nothing? The one you used like bail on the night a man knocked and you did not open?"

The confessional door across the nave banged once. Every head turned except Sister Helena's.

"Eyes on me," she commanded without looking back, and somehow, they obeyed.

The chair rose an inch. Leather sang in buckles. Candleflames leaned toward the levitation as if flame were metal and the girl were magnet. The monstrance shivered. The reliquary rang, a glassy ping like a fork flicked against crystal.

Sister Helena pressed the crucifix to Ashlyn's brow. Smoke snaked from skin. The scream that came was in three registers at once: a child's ragged shriek, a woman's long high keen, a bass under-note that made teeth ache.

"Fiat lux?" breathed the layered voice when the scream broke. "Then why do you love the dark?" Its eyes hid their black shine behind lids half-closed in a look Father Michael had seen on parish bullies and a few bishops: gracious, pitying. "You pray in the dark even at noon."

He nearly dropped the crucifix. He caught it. He did not answer.

"Exorcízo te…" Sister Helena drove on, each syllable another hammer. "…imperat tibi Deus."

"Imperat tibi Deus," the mouth chimed back, delighted, as if the sentence were a nursery rhyme. The organ gave one long dissonant moan without fingers on keys. A hairline crack spidered the blue of the north transept window; dust sifted from somewhere high and old and fell soft as ash on Daniel's sleeve.

The first assault had begun in earnest.

Scripture, Bulls, and Blasphemy

"Ego sum lux mundi," Daniel intoned, Gospel held like a shield.

"Light," the voice purred. "Your favorite toy." It slipped into a baritone that carried the old Roman cadence.

"Summis desiderantes affectibus, Quo primum tempore, oh, let me speak your paper to you, scholar," it said toward Elias.

"Let me bind you with your own thread."

"I know those words," Elias said hoarsely. "I know what they've done."

"Do you?" The grin widened. "You think knowing saves you. It saved no one. It fed me."

Nora clutched her rosary. A bead snapped and clicked along the marble like a tiny knuckle bone. She didn't chase it. She tucked the cross into her fist and held.

"Exi," Sister Helena said, English under the Latin, blade under club. "Leave."

"I will," the mouth breathed, sweet as a promise. "When I am finished."

The organ moaned again. The chandeliers trembled though no air stirred. The brazier's coal leaned into its own glow and decided to burn brighter.

The Knife to the Heart: Sister Helena

The voice softened. "Sister?"

Sister Helena did not answer. She did not drop her gaze from the crucifix. She could not stop hearing.

"Sister," the voice tried again, small. A boy's voice. The exact pitch. The exact breath between hermana and por favor.

"You prayed and I got better. Mama kissed your hands. We told everyone. Milagro."

Smoke from the brazier suddenly smelled like Oaxaca in the late afternoon, heat in the blood, diesel from a bus, the sweetness of rotting fruit in a market alley.

"And then I died harder," the voice said. "Thank you."

Sister Helena's beads slipped. Her fingers grabbed air and got nothing. The rosary jumped and hit marble and scattered in a little hail of Hail Marys. She closed her hand on the empty cord and felt the old rage rise, at herself, at the lie that had used her prayer like a ladder.

"You opened the door," said the mouth, maternal now, her voice, the boy's mother, heavy with gratitude first, then with grief. "And then you watched him break."

"Enough," Sister Helena said. It came out small because grief compresses sound.

"Sister Helena." Father Michael's voice, low, near, human, found her. Not Sister. Not Exorcist. "With me."

Her eyes snapped to his. He didn't comfort. He didn't advise. He was just there. She closed her hand on that presence like a swimmer grabs a rope.

She lifted the crucifix again.

"Imperat tibi Deus Filius…"

The Knife to the Bone: Elias and Daniel

The grin took on tenderness and contempt in equal measure.

"Son," it said, a father's voice that should have made Elias a boy again and instead made him a bad man at a podium.

Elias' chest stopped for one beat. He remembered Daniel at eight with a too-large cassock and a joy so unguarded he had been ashamed to look. He remembered saying clever things in rooms that smelled of coffee and dust while his boy waited for him outside a door with stained glass that had made him weep without knowing why.

"Look at him praying, the voice crooned to Elias. He did what you wouldn't. He became the thing that made you feel small."

Daniel stepped in front of his father because he was built that way.

"Talk to me," he said. "Not him."

"Oh, we will," said the shadow, and his own voice came back out of the girl's mouth, perfect cadence, perfect rasp, the one he used to try not to cry.

"You wanted to win. You wanted to pray where he could see the edge of your sword."

"Daniel," Elias said, and the word creaked, rusted from disuse in the world where fathers speak to sons without adding a thesis.

"I'm here."

The demon snorted through the child's nose.

"You're late."

"I'm here," Elias said again, and the second time he didn't apologize with it.

The Parents: Love as a Weapon

Nora's voice was a thread fraying against her teeth.

"My girl. My girl." Every time the mouth mocked, she said it. Every time the shadow tried to throw a story, she told a different one. She hummed a lullaby wrong on purpose so no echo could find it.

"Let me sleep," the mouth said in Ashlyn's real timbre for one treacherous second. "Let me sleep forever."

"No," Nora said. "You will wake and eat cereal in my kitchen. You will leave your shoes in the hallway and I'll trip on them and curse. That is the story."

Sean gripped the pew until the wood complained.

"Take me," he said, because fathers are stupid with love and it is their best stupidity.

"But I already did," the shadow sighed through the girl's mouth, and it spoke in Sean's own pub-night voice, the one he hated, the one a bottle used when it wore him. "Every night you left her crying and I seduced you out the door." He bent double and did not break. Nora put a hand on the back of his neck and he remembered to breathe.

The Cathedral Answers

Something high in the ribs of the roof cracked with the little noise old timber makes when it remembers storms. The stained glass in the north transept finally surrendered a sliver: a blue shard fell and struck marble and sang and became dust. The organ gave not a note but a breath, like a whale surfacing.

The monstrance seemed brighter though no one touched it. Not glitter. Weight. The Presence pressing outward the way heat presses from a living body in winter.

The brazier roared without more charcoal. The smoke lost its sweetness and took on a clean bite, like paper burning that has written itself out.

"Ecce crucem Domini," Sister Helena said, and splashed holy water, and the droplets did not sizzle this time. They simply vanished at contact, as if drunk greedily.

The Folium Wakes

Elias had kept the linen over the glass because superstition is simply ritual half-remembered. Now, as the air thickened and the girl's body bucked, the cloth shifted. He hadn't touched it. It shifted like breath. He drew it aside before his cowardice could say don't.

The blood-letters were not letters anymore. They were verbs. They moved. They crawled across the page like ants forming and reforming columns. They blinked out and reappeared in other orders. Candlelight glossed their edges and gave them the sheen of wet.

Father Michael read before he could refuse himself.

"Non repetere verba. Non servare ordinem. Loquere ex corde."

"Do not repeat the words. Do not keep the order. Speak from the heart."

The scream that came scoured the nave. The rose window shuddered but held. The demon's three voices collided and made a fourth that sounded like a crowd realizing at once that a bridge is collapsing under them.

"Close it!" Sister Helena snapped.

"We have to see," Elias said, and he hated his own hunger and obeyed it anyway.

The words flowed into another line.

"Umbra Dei ligatur non lumine, sed fide."

Umbra Dei is bound not by light, but by faith.

The mouth spit like an animal.

"Do not read me," the shadow snarled. "I read you."

"Then read this," Father Michael said softly, and his own surprise at his courage tasted like blood.

The Second Wave: The Past Brought Present

The chair lifted clean off the floor, three inches, six, a foot, held in air by nothing anyone's eyes could name. The straps thrummed like plucked strings. Ashlyn's limbs contorted backward in angles no muscle could endorse. Her jaw unhinged one click farther than bone should allow. A column of black smoke poured from her mouth and climbed, slick and ribboned, toward the vaulting.

The confessional door banged open and shut and open and shut and a voice without air behind it said, Father, I'm in here, I'm in here, and a knock came from inside Father Michael's chest, three knocks, evenly spaced. He staggered. He tasted floodwater. He saw his mother's hand on a hospital sheet in the same instant and realized grief and guilt share nerves.

Sister Helena heard the Oaxaca mother, qué hiciste, hermana, and then she heard her own voice, younger, eager, reading a martyr's line aloud in a convent archive: I burn still. She wanted to bite her own tongue in half and spit out the part that had said it. She wanted to stand in that old room and strike the lamp down and let the moths have darkness back. She steadied the crucifix instead.

Elias heard Daniel as a boy praying the Our Father with the ferocious enunciation children use when they are afraid of getting something wrong and he wanted to apologize, and he wanted to grab the book and cram pages into the brazier until flame had eaten what flame could not eat, and he wanted to kneel, and he did none of those three.

He whispered, "I am here," and the whisper belonged to this room, not to a memory.

Daniel heard his own voice when he had said I want to be a priest so at least one of us will love God in this family, and he wanted to punch that boy and hug him and tell him love is not a bar-fight you win by being the last man standing. He lifted the Gospel and read another line.

"Et verbum caro factum est."

The smoke twitched. The shadow hates incarnation. It cannot eat what refuses metaphor.

Blood, Ash, Fire

"Now," Sister Helena said, and it was not theatrical. It was a carpenter saying now when two men have muscled a beam into position and one must hammer before gravity remembers.

Daniel took the brazier. He carried it around the chair once, and the flame made a low sound you could mistake for chant if you needed to. He moved slow, procession, not panic, and the heat licked his knuckles and did not own him.

Sister Helena dipped her thumb into the ash and drew a cross on Ashlyn's brow. The grit left a gray-black print on her skin.

"You are dust," she said, and turned one word, "and to truth you shall return." The shadow flinched at the swap. Lies prefer you promise men to dust; truth is a place they choke.

Father Michael took the small knife. He didn't look at the old scar. He drew the new line exactly over it. The cut was not beautiful. It didn't need to be. Blood welled and made his palm a tiny red lake. He smeared it on the crucifix and the metal took the heat of it and wore it.

"Out of the depths," he said, not reciting but testifying, "I cry to You, O Lord." The You was not rhetoric; it landed. He did not know how he knew that. He knew it anyway.

The smoke convulsed like something gagging. The chair slammed back to marble and the sound ricocheted through the nave. The organ coughed out three notes that wanted to be a hymn and failed beautifully.

A Priest Opens a Door

The confessional door knocked. Not banged. Knocked: three gentle raps with the politeness of someone who still believes in being invited as he drowns.

Father Michael walked to it. Not fast. Not slowly. He opened the door. The interior smelled like old wood and fabric warm from bodies. He sat inside and closed the door most of the way and through the lattice said the sentence that has saved more men than Latin: "Bless me, Father, for I have sinned."

He answered himself, God answering through him, ridiculous and true, aloud, so the demon would have to hear:

"God, the Father of mercies, through the death and resurrection of His Son, has reconciled the world to Himself and sent the Holy Spirit among us for the forgiveness of sins. I absolve you.

He felt foolish. He felt like a man opening an umbrella in a hurricane. He felt strong. He stood and came back out. The knocking had stopped. The shadow had one less mouth.

"Again," Sister Helena said, borrowing the demon's word and taking the teeth out of it.

The Forbidden Line

The Folium squirmed to a halt under glass. The letters held, as if they had spent themselves. A final line

glowed with the dull shine blood finds when candlelight
and breath agree on it:

"Non in lumine, sed in fide, te conjuro exi."

"Not in light, but in faith, I conjure you to him."

Sister Helena read it with Father Michael at the
exact same breath. They hadn't planned to. The voices
met mid-air and braided. The sentence did not look
brave on paper. It sounded like stone thrown at a wolf.

"Non in lumine, sed in fide, te conjuro exi!"

"Not in light, but in faith, I conjure you to him."

The monstrance's rays did not turn into fireworks.
They did what rays do: they pointed, and what they
pointed at could not pretend in that direction anymore.
The brazier's flame did not leap theatrically to the
vaulting; it burned like real fire, total, hungry, honest.
The candles did not explode; they steadied.

Ashlyn levitated again, higher, then higher. Her
arms were pulled out to her sides by nothing and made
the shape of a cross because the world loves its cruel
symmetries. Her mouth opened wider and the smoke
that came was not smoke anymore; it was a thing. It had
the sheen of oil and the speed of wind and the malice of
echo deprived of a throat. It threw itself at the rose
window and struck and shuddered and gathered and
threw itself again.

"Not faith," the chorus hissed, foundering. "Not
faith! Faith burns!"

Father Michael answered with the only honest thing in him. "Then burn."

Sister Helena and he spoke again, as if the sentence were made to be said twice and no more:

"Non in lumine, sed in fide, te conjuro exi!"

"Not in light, but in faith, I conjure you to him."

The shadow convulsed and tore free of the girl's body, no ripping of meat, no gore, just a vacating, a sudden fact of space where it had been. It slammed itself against the monstrance's invisible circumference and howled and the howl made every spider in the rafters go still. It clawed the rose window and the glass held. It rose, a column of writhing not-light, and struck something no one could see and came apart like a handful of midnight thrown against noon.

For the length of a breath the nave went absolutely lightless. No candle. No window. No phone screen. The kind of dark in which people see themselves.

A single flame relit on the altar. Then another. Then a chain along the rail. Then chandeliers. Light returned like men returning from war, one at a time, carrying each other.

Aftermath: The Sound of Human Breath

Ashlyn collapsed into the chair so completely it was as if the wood had claimed her and was now giving her back. Her head tipped to one side. Her lips moved, uncertain in their own shape. Nora was there before anyone else, hands on her child's cheeks, on her brow, on her shoulders, as if sheer human contact could hold a soul in. Sean's massive hand covered both of theirs.

Ashlyn's eyes opened. They were brown. They were wet. They were confused. They were a girl's eyes in the first seconds after waking from a far-too-long nightmare.

"Mom?" It was so small.

Nora made a sound no word owns.

"Yes. Yes, my love." She kissed Ashlyn's forehead. "We're here."

Sean pressed his forehead to Ashlyn's hair and shook like a building giving up its last stress.

"I'm here, kiddo," he whispered into her scalp. "I'm here. I'm not going anywhere."

Father Michael dropped the crucifix, not from weakness but because he had never learned how to hold joy and wood at the same time. He sat on the first step and bent forward and cried. Not pretty. The kind of cry men do when a tendon snaps. It lasted seconds. It lasted years.

Sister Helena crossed herself and turned away because some mercies should not be watched. She picked up three of her scattered beads and did not string them yet. She simply held them and let her hand know their shape again.

Elias lowered the Folium's glass and covered it with linen and tied the twine with hands that shook less now. "Not by words," he said aloud, which for a scholar is a vow like poverty. He looked at Daniel and did not have a speech.

"Pray with me," he said instead, and Daniel did, and their Our Father was ugly and beautiful and half-out-of-synch and exactly right.

The confessional door stood open a hair. Father Michael walked to it later, when breath had become common again, and he rested his palm against it without flinching. "I am here," he said to the empty inside, and the emptiness did not mock him; it received the sentence like stone receives heat, slowly, truly.

The Cathedral Remembers

The cathedral breathed out. Timber settled with relieved ticks. The organ made a little sound like an old man clearing his throat. The broken blue shard on the floor caught a candle and threw a tiny ocean onto a patch of marble and then went dull.

Somewhere above, a pigeon that had sheltered between stone and lead during the shriek shuffled its feet and decided to stay quiet awhile longer.

The air smelled like wax and ash and sweat and something clean.

The rose window let dawn touch the nave, thin at first, then more. Morning found the monstrance and put a simple, secular light on it that did not cancel the other kind.

Nora and Sean unbuckled the straps with hands that couldn't not shake. Buckles are stubborn when they have done grim work; these yielded like men surrendering. They lifted Ashlyn and she folded into them, not limp anymore, just tired.

Daniel and Elias stood shoulder to shoulder and did not speak. Their silence did not ache like before. It rested.

Sister Helena turned her bead horde over in her palm and found the broken cord end and smiled a little because she would mend it and she had always liked mending better than buying new.

Father Michael looked up at the crucifix and did not ask. He said thank you and meant it and it hurt and healed in the same mouthful.

Bishop Shaw appeared from the shadows where he had kept out of sight because he had decided the Church best serves sometimes by not narrating herself in the moment. He made the sign of the cross over everyone and did not give a speech.

"Rest," he said. "Eat," he added. He did not say there will be forms. There would be, and he would burn half of them.

The Last Whisper and the Last Word

It would be a lie to say the shadow did not try a final trick.

As they gathered, a thread of sound moved through the nave, not from the chair, not from the rafters, not from any single mouth. It said, almost conversationally, almost kind: "I burn still."

Sister Helena went very still, like a woman listening for a snake in grass. The line had been a hook in her ribs for decades. She had sharpened herself on it. She had bled on it. She lifted her chin.

"Not here," she said, simple, flat. "Not in her. Not in us."

Father Michael lifted the crucifix again, not to brandish, but to weigh.

"Be gone," he said, English, nothing fancy. "And do not return."

The whisper had nowhere left to perch. It fled the way mist flees when sun commits to rising.

The cathedral kept the silence like a box keeps a keepsake. Outside, Boston realized the hour and turned on coffee makers and radios. Ambulances woke up and pretended they had not rested. Buses sighed.

Inside, faith smelled like ash and sweat and beeswax and human breath. It sounded like a mother's laugh through tears and a father's curse turned into a prayer halfway out of his mouth. It looked like a monstrance holding still while darkness flailed itself to pieces.

They stood a while and then they moved, because bodies must move after miracles or else miracles become museums. They gathered the glass chips. They straightened the candles. They ate the peanut-butter sandwiches someone had not thrown away in the rectory kitchen. They said little.

Ashlyn slept against Nora's shoulder, breathing like a person asleep and not like a thing possessed.

Sister Helena paused at the threshold and looked back once, not to consecrate the memory but to inventory: the chair in silhouette; the ash bowl scuffed with thumb; the brazier's coal dead and honest; the linen covering the book; the blue shard the sweep had missed glinting like a note in a margin. She took in the scene like she would take in a field after harvest: not empty, but finished.

"Again?" Father Michael asked softly, a man who has learned the world will ask him to keep showing up.

"When it comes," Sister Helena said. "And it will." She did not dread saying it. Saying it felt like telling the truth to someone you trust.

They stepped into Boston's ordinary morning. Sun came off police cruisers and puddles with the same flare. Somewhere a Yankee fan laughed too loud and a Red Sox fan swore with love. The city did what cities do. The cathedral held what cathedrals hold.

And beneath the vaulting ribs where praying has worn grooves into air, the words remained, not as ink, not as smoke, but as lived thing:

Non in lumine, sed in fide, te conjuro exi.

Not in light, but in faith, I conjure you to him.

Chapter 23

Ashes and Silence

"Ecclesia est lumen, sed umbra sequitur semper."
The Church is light, but the shadow always follows.

The silence after battle was heavier than the noise. No shrieks, no smoke tearing from a child's throat, no hymn mocked and twisted. Only breathing. Human breathing.

Ashlyn Sullivan's chest rose and fell, shallow at first, then steadier. The sound was fragile, like parchment handled too many times, but it was real. Her lashes fluttered against her pale cheeks. She stirred, her head lolling slightly against her mother's arm.

Nora gasped as though that faint motion was thunder. Her hands trembled as she cupped her daughter's face.

"Ash... sweetheart? Can you hear me?"

For a long heartbeat there was nothing. Then her lips parted, a whisper catching in her throat.

"Mom?"

It was her voice not layered, not distorted, not stolen. Only hers.

Nora broke, sobbing into her daughter's hair, rocking her as though she were an infant again. Tears streaked her face, fell onto Ashlyn's temple, mingled with sweat and the faint trace of ash still clinging to her skin.

Sean leaned close, his broad shoulders shaking. He kissed the crown of her head, his voice breaking on the words.

"We've got you, Ash. We've got you."

His arms folded around both his wife and daughter, enclosing them in a circle of grief and joy so fierce it could hardly be distinguished.

Weak But Alive

Ashlyn blinked again, her eyes unfocused at first, then slowly sharpening. They were brown. Not black, not rolling white only brown, dulled with exhaustion but alive.

Her throat worked as she tried to speak. Nora hushed her quickly, brushing her hair back from her damp forehead.

"Shh, love. Don't try yet. Just breathe."

Still, Ashlyn managed a rasp.

"Cold."

Sean pulled off his own jacket and wrapped it around her shoulders. His hands lingered there, unwilling to let go, as though the moment he loosened his grip she might vanish again.

"You're safe," Nora whispered fiercely. "You're safe now. Nothing's going to touch you."

Ashlyn's brow creased faintly.

"The... voices..."

Her parents exchanged a look, pain flickering through their relief. Nora pressed her lips to her daughter's temple.

"Gone," she lied softly. "Gone for good."

Sister Helena, standing a few paces away, did not correct her. She simply closed her eyes and let the family's moment hold. Truth could come later.

The Family Weeps

Tears came easily now, spilling without shame. Sean wept like he had not wept since his brother Patrick's burial, his great frame shaking silently. Nora wept in gulps and gasps, her sobs mingling with murmured thanks to the Virgin, to Christ, to anyone listening.

Ashlyn wept too, though hers were quieter, softer. They came without memory of why she had to cry, only the body's release after too much torment.

Their weeping filled the nave more beautifully than the organ ever had. It was not song, but it was truth, and the cathedral, weary as its stones were, seemed to bow around the sound, keeping it safe within its walls.

Elias turned away, throat tight, giving them privacy. Daniel stood beside him, and for the first time in years, Elias did not flinch from his son's nearness. He let the sight of family whole, imperfect, still breathing settle into him.

Shadows of What Was Lost

Even in the joy, shadows lingered. The straps of the oak chair lay loose and dangling, blackened where smoke had touched them. Ash still smudged the marble floor. The brazier's coals glowed faintly, embering like a wound not yet scabbed.

Ashlyn's wrists bore red welts where leather had bitten deep. Her neck showed faint bruises in the pattern of unseen hands, and on her brow, Sister Helena's ash-cross marked her still, a scarlet reminder of the fight waged in blood and faith.

Nora's tears thickened as she saw them. She kissed each welt as though her lips could erase them, muttering broken apologies for things she had never caused.

Sean rested his head against Ashlyn's and whispered, "You're stronger than me, girl. Stronger than me."

The Fragile Calm

Minutes stretched in the fragile calm. The family clung together, weeping, rocking, whispering thanks and comfort. The candles burned low, their wax dripping onto silver holders. Dawn light slipped through the broken rose window, scattering across the marble in pale gold.

Father Michael stood nearby, crucifix still clutched in his hand, but for once it felt lighter than ever before. His chest heaved with exhaustion. Sweat streaked his face. Yet beneath it all, beneath the trembling and the guilt still gnawing, something steadier had kindled.

He watched Nora cradle her daughter and thought: This is prayer answered. Not because I deserved it, but because He is still here.

The thought startled him. For years he had prayed into what felt like silence. Now, for the first time since his mother's hospital bed, he believed the silence might not mean absence.

Sister Helena exhaled slowly, shoulders sagging. Her crucifix lowered, her hand trembling with release. She whispered a psalm under her breath, words she had long since worn smooth from use.

She glanced toward the altar, where she knew she would go when the family no longer needed eyes upon them. There, she would kneel, and perhaps the silence would tell her whether she was forgiven.

Ashlyn Speaks

Ashlyn stirred again, opening her eyes fully. Her gaze shifted from her mother to her father, then to the faces gathered beyond. Her voice was rough, cracked, but audible.

"What... happened?"

Nora stroked her hair, eyes flooding anew.

"You were sick, love, but you're safe now. Father Michael and Sister Helena... they helped us."

Ashlyn's eyes drifted to the priest and the nun. For a heartbeat, fear flickered there, some shadow of memory she couldn't name, but it passed, leaving only weary curiosity

"Thank you," she whispered.

Father Michael swallowed hard, his throat thick.

"Don't thank me," he said softly. "Thank Him." He glanced toward the crucifix above the altar, his words as much for himself as for her.

Sister Helena bowed her head. She did not accept thanks, not yet, not when her heart still burned with guilt.

The Weight of Survival

Ashlyn's eyelids drooped again. Exhaustion tugged her downward, pulling her toward sleep. Nora eased her head against her shoulder, humming softly, a lullaby she had not sung in years. Sean kept one hand on her arm, grounding them both.

The family wept still, though quieter now, sobs fading into sniffles and deep breaths. They had wept until their throats were raw, until they had nothing left but the weight of survival.

Sister Helena stepped back, giving them space. Her own eyes brimmed but did not spill. She had wept in Oaxaca. She had sworn never to again, but tonight, as dawn brushed the cathedral, she felt tears press harder than ever. She swallowed them down. There would be time at the altar.

Father Michael pressed a hand against the pew, grounding himself. His legs trembled with fatigue, but inside him something had steadied. The hollow ache that had haunted his prayers was not gone, but it was filled now with something different: presence, unseen but undeniable.

He breathed, and for once, the breath was prayer.

The family held together in a knot of arms and tears. Ashlyn, slipping into sleep, still clutched her father's sleeve with a weak, instinctive grip. Nora's hand moved rhythmically through her daughter's hair, rocking gently, as if the motion itself might keep her soul anchored in the world.

Father Michael let them be. His gaze lifted to the crucifix above the altar the carved Christ hanging in agony, wood darkened by years of incense smoke and candle soot. His hands trembled, still stained with blood from his own palm.

For years, he had carried the weight of unanswered prayers, the hollow ache of believing words spoken into an empty sky. The confessional had haunted him: the knocking he had not answered, the addict who had drowned alone while he pretended the noise was the storm.

Now, watching Ashlyn breathe, he felt the weight shift. Not vanish, but move. His failure was real, but it was not the last word. For the first time, he believed that the silence of God was not abandonment it was mystery.

He pressed his bleeding palm to his chest. The pain grounded him.

"Lord," he whispered, voice raw, "I believe. Help my unbelief."

The words broke him open. He sank to the pew, bowing his head, and let the tears fall freely. He did not fight them. For once, he allowed himself to be seen weeping.

Sister Helena's Path

Sister Helena had held herself steady during the ritual, a soldier of faith standing unbroken, but now, as the dawn light spread across the nave, her body sagged. The crucifix in her hand felt heavier than iron. The psalm in her throat cracked into silence.

She turned toward the altar. Step by step, she approached, her beads still loose in her hand, the cord frayed and broken. She had picked up what she could, but some beads remained lost on the marble, scattered like bones.

She knelt before the altar, knees pressing into the cold stone. Her crucifix lay across the corporal, its silver dulled by ash and blood. She lowered her forehead to the wood of the altar rail and whispered, "Forgive me."

Her voice shook. Memories flooded her: the boy in Oaxaca writhing in convulsions, the mother's cries, the whispered word Milagro that had turned to ash in her ears. The martyr's line she had once read aloud, I burn still, now echoing through decades.

"Forgive me for the doors I opened. Forgive me for the child I failed. Forgive me for praying when I did not understand what I was calling."

Her shoulders shook as sobs finally claimed her. She pressed her beads to her lips. "Do not let this be in vain."

For the first time in years, she allowed herself to be broken before the altar, not as an exorcist, not as a soldier of faith, but simply as a daughter begging her father's mercy.

The Scholar and His Son

Across the nave, Elias Kearns sat heavily in a pew, the Folium Obscurum wrapped and sealed beside him. His hands rested on his knees, palms upward, as though he were waiting for something to be placed in them.

Daniel sat beside him. The silence between them was not jagged as it had been in years past. It was softer now, worn down by fire and fear.

Elias swallowed hard. "I nearly lost you," he said quietly.

Daniel glanced at him, then back toward the altar. "You didn't. I'm here."

The words were simple, but they cracked something open in Elias's chest. He turned, really looking at his son the lines in his face, the steadiness in his hands, the faith in his eyes. For years, Elias had sneered at such faith, called it blind, called it weak.

Now, after the night they had endured, he could not call it anything but strength.

"Daniel," he said, voice low, "I am proud of you."

His son's eyes flicked to him again, a faint, cautious smile tugging at his lips.

"That's a start," he said softly.

And Elias, for the first time in decades, allowed himself to smile back.

The Family's Vigil

Nora and Sean had not let go of their daughter. They held her still, even as her breathing deepened into the rhythm of exhausted sleep. They whispered prayers over her, words old and new, sometimes jumbled together but always fierce with love.

Sean kissed her temple and murmured, "I would have traded places with you. I would have gone instead."

Nora hushed him gently.

"She's here. That's all that matters."

They stayed kneeling long after their knees ached, unwilling to break the fragile circle of their reunion. Every time Ashlyn shifted, every time she sighed in her sleep, they tightened their hold.

They had lost Patrick, carried his coffin, kissed a cold forehead. They would not lose Ashlyn. Not now.

The Cathedral Holds

The cathedral had witnessed violence in the night
glass shattering, wood splintering, voices twisted into
mockery. Now it held silence.

Ash clung to the marble floor, streaked with
footprints and beads of water. The broken rose window
let dawn spill in freely, painting gold across the altar rail.
Candles guttered low, their wax dripping in rivulets
down brass holders.

The air smelled of smoke and sweat, salt from tears,
faint sweetness from the last of the incense.

The silence was not empty. It was full, full of
breath, of relief, of grief uncoiled. The cathedral cradled
it all, as it had for generations, as it would for
generations yet.

Father Michael Renewed

Father Michael rose slowly from the pew, wiping
tears from his cheeks with the back of his hand. He felt
raw, scraped clean, as though something inside him had
been torn open and left to bleed light.

He approached the altar, standing near Sister Helena but giving her space. He bowed his head, crucifix still in hand.

"I thought I had lost You," he whispered. "All those years of silence. All the prayers that seemed to go nowhere. I thought I was only speaking to myself."

His grip on the crucifix tightened. "But You were here. Even in silence, you were here. Even in my failures. Even in the confessional I never opened."

He pressed the crucifix to his chest. His voice steadied. "I will not run again."

The words surprised him, but they felt true. For the first time in years, he believed. Not because he had proven anything, not because he was strong, but because grace had met him in the ashes and silence.

Sister Helena's Answer

Beside him, Sister Helena lifted her head from the altar rail. Her face was wet with tears, but her eyes were steady. She looked at Father Michael and nodded once, silent agreement.

Her own prayer had not brought a voice, no sudden thunderbolt of forgiveness, but the weight she carried had shifted, as did his. She felt the edges of redemption pressing against her, not yet fully realized, but possible.

She touched the broken beads in her hand, rolling them between her fingers.

"We are forgiven," she murmured, not to him, not to herself, but into the silence.

And for the first time in decades, she believed it might be true.

The Ashes and the Silence

The night had left its scars. The floor was marked, the glass shattered, the wood singed. The people were weary, shaken, hollowed.

And yet, in the stillness of dawn, something sacred lingered.

Ashlyn breathed softly in her mother's arms. Father Michael stood renewed before the altar. Sister Heléna knelt, scarred but lifted. Elias and Daniel sat side by side without bitterness.

The ashes on the floor remained, but the silence above them was not void. It was presence.

The bells of the city began to toll the hour. Morning light spread across the nave.

Nora kissed her daughter's brow again. Sean whispered thanks through his tears.

Father Michael made the sign of the cross, his hand steady. Sister Helena closed her eyes in prayer. Elias folded the Folium Obscurum away for the last time.

Daniel touched his father's shoulder and left his hand there.

The cathedral kept its silence.

And in that silence, faith lived.

Chapter 24

The Vatican's Shadow

*"In novissimo aevo umbra resurget, cum ipsa Ecclesia nomen
eius invocat."*
*In the last age, the Shadow shall rise again, when the Church
itself calls to him.*
— *Liber Obscura, Fragmentum 311*

The first thing Ashlyn noticed when they turned
onto O'Reilly Street was how ordinary everything
looked. The elm out front held a sleeve of early leaves.
Mr. Kelly's recycling bin still leaned cockeyed near the
curb, as if the Tuesday truck had shrugged at it. A red
bicycle, the neighbor kid's, lay half on the lawn, half on
the sidewalk, defying gravity with the stubbornness of
youth.

Inside the car, no one spoke. Sean drove with both
hands white-knuckled on the wheel, as if steering
through glass. Nora kept a steady palm on Ashlyn's
knee, the way she had done when Ash was five and cars
meant naps. Daniel and Elias followed in Elias's aging
sedan, headlights ghosting through the Autumn light.

They did not go fast. You don't rush after a miracle;
you don't jostle it. You carry it as if it can still spill.

At the curb, Sean eased into park and turned off the
engine. The silence that followed had the strange

loudness of a church after the final chord. He looked over his shoulder.

"You ready, kiddo?"

Ashlyn's eyes were open but muzzy, pupils slow, the brown of them blurred with fatigue.

"I think so." Her voice still rasped, as if she'd swallowed smoke.

He lifted her gently, a careful heft that pulled at an old baseball injury but didn't complain. Nora opened the front door, awkward with keys and shaking hands, and the house breathed them in the sweet stale of laundry and dinners and a life that had been paused too long.

They put Ashlyn on the sofa because somehow a bed felt too much like closing your eyes forever. The living room had not changed since the last normal morning: the framed school pictures on the shelf (Ashlyn at ten, Ashlyn at twelve with braces; Patrick in his dress blues, the frame braided in a thin black ribbon), the crocheted throw blanket Nora's aunt had made before her hands began to ache, the Red Sox schedule magnetized to the corner of the TV.

Nora pulled the throw up to Ashlyn's chin.

"Water?"

Ash nodded. The nod nearly knocked her out. She shut her eyes while Nora hurried to the kitchen, the sound of the tap loud as a river.

Sean sat on the coffee table, too big for it, the wood creaking under the question of him. He stared as if making sure his mind had not invented her shape. When she opened her eyes again, he blurted, too gruff, "We're getting a new lock for your window, and I'm moving the bat back under the bed."

She smiled, a small, honest crook of the mouth.

"Like I'm five."

"Exactly like you're five." His smile cracked into relief. "We'll grow you back to fourteen slowly."

Nora returned with the glass. Ashlyn sipped, the water tasting like something earned. She coughed once, hard, and they both jumped, haunted by the sounds her throat had made the night before. Ash waved them off, embarrassed by their terror.

"It's just... water," she said, and the fact that just water made three people tear up was proof that ordinary things are the holiest.

Daniel and Elias came in quietly, unsure of their welcome in this room that belonged to one family's morning. Nora hugged them both anyway, the professor a little stiff, the deacon trying not to look like he needed the embrace too.

"Tea?" she offered automatically, because Irish houses default to boiling water in defense against grief.

"Please," Elias said, as if tea might be a sacrament he had overlooked in all his reading. Daniel helped him out of his coat and then stood by the mantle; hands tucked into his sleeves. The room smelled of lemon cleaner and candle wax. He let it fill his lungs.

There were a thousand things to do that no one could do yet. A doctor to call. A neighbor to inform. The broken crucifix to rehang in the hallway. The sigils on Ashlyn's bedroom wall to face and then paint over, or not paint over, and that argument could wait.

For now, there was the couch and the blanket, and hands, and the sound of a kettle finding its voice.

Nora ran her fingers through Ash's hair, parting it the way she did when checking for summer lice years ago.

"It's really you," she whispered, as if there were versions that weren't.

Ashlyn's lips trembled.

"Do I... say sorry? For... everything?"

"No," Sean said, maybe too quickly. He cleared his throat. "No, love. Not one damn thing."

She nodded, and even that small assent made her eyelids droop. She slept, finally, not the false collapse of possession, but the heavy honest sleep of a body that has been held too long and let go.

They watched her as if watching could be a form of guard duty. The kettle clicked off. Nora poured tea without leaving the doorway, unwilling to turn her back. Elias took the mug with both hands, the heat a tether to the room. Daniel stood sentinel at the window, looking out at O'Reilly Street as if the street itself might try to steal her.

After a while, Sean exhaled, long, a breath he had apparently been saving since the day Patrick left for Iraq. He rested his head in his hands.

"Do we tell anyone?" he asked, voice muffled.

Nora wiped her eyes with the corner of her sleeve.

"Tell them what? That our daughter was... sick and now she's better?"

"That we had a miracle," he said, as if daring the word to stand between them.

"Let's keep it small," Nora said. "Let's keep it ours. The world can have the Red Sox. I'll take my girl."

Sean laughed, a tired sound.

"The Sox will break your heart."

"They already did," she whispered, and they both smiled because pain with an old local joke on it was the only flavor of pain they could swallow.

On the mantle, Patrick's picture caught a blade of morning and threw it back. Sean reached up and straightened the frame the small amount that made it right.

"Thank you," he murmured to the boy he could no longer hold, and some part of him believed the thanks found its mark.

The Walk

Father Michael did not go straight back to the rectory. After Ensure-strength coffee in the Sullivan kitchen that made his hands tremble less and his mouth feel both alive and punished, he stepped outside into the thin Boston morning and found his shoes had chosen the long way around the block.

His palm still ached where he had opened it. He did not bandage it. He wanted the sting. It reminded him of truth in a way no sentence could. The city wore its everyday: a mail carrier rolling his cart as if the wheels never squeaked; a couple in scrubs arguing tenderly about nothing at all; a man walking a dog who acted like he had invented grass.

Father Michael breathed, and the breath did not bounce. It went somewhere. He could not explain it. He did not try. Some gifts you do not unwrap with words.

He passed a corner store where the radio announced morning scores and traffic and the kind of tragedy that becomes small in the mouth of a DJ. The Yankees had done what they do. The city grieved and moved and went to work anyway

He stopped outside the Cathedral of the Holy Cross before he realized he had come. The great doors still wore last night. The custodians had swept most of the glass. The blue sliver he had noticed in the aisle remained, glinting like a stubborn idea. He bent and picked it up. It was light in his palm, a feather of glass. He tucked it into his pocket with the care of a man carrying a relic.

Inside, the nave sat in that clean wreck a church knows after a vigil: wax runs hardened, ashes smudged, the air not yet ready to release incense. He walked up the center aisle slowly, letting the space reset his bones to their old setting.

The chair had been moved against the transept wall. It looked like furniture again, and he felt a flash of anger that made him ashamed, anger at the chair for being a chair, at wood for being innocent. He set his hand on the armrest anyway and spoke a word he had not spoken to objects in a long time: "Thank you."

In the east transept, the confessional door stood open as if it, too, were tired of keeping secrets. He went inside and shut it to the width he had left last night and sat. The wood smelled like what it always smells like: old varnish, damp, a thousand colognes baked into grain, the salt of fear. He heard only his own breath. He did not expect a knock.

"Bless me, Father," he said to the lattice, because now the sentence tasted like bread and not like failure. He did not speak the rest aloud. Some confessions are between a man and the One listening, with no scribe and no witness and no demon invited to the hearing. When he finished, he stepped back into the transept and bowed his head, not as prelude to more words but because sometimes bodies do what they learned before minds did.

On the sanctuary step, Sister Helena knelt. He had not seen her slip past him. The light along her profile could have been a blade or a blessing, depending on what a person wanted to see. She held her beads without moving them, thumb resting against a cracked decade. Her shoulders did not shake. Some people weep like rivers; some like dew evaporating as it forms.

"Do you need the space alone?" Father Michael asked softly.

"No," she said, and the word was not dismissal. "Stay."

He sat on the lowest step. For a while they said nothing, and the silence worked on them like hands.

Finally, Sister Helena spoke without looking up.

"When I was a girl, I read a line I shouldn't have. I built a life of discipline around the fear that my curiosity had lit a fuse no one could snuff out." She glanced at him now; the glance did not seek absolution. "Last night, the fuse burned to ash. Not because of me. Because of Him."

Father Michael nodded.

"I told Him I would not run," he said, as if reporting to her mattered in the same way it did to God.

"That was the first time in a long time I made a vow without bargaining."

"The first time in a long time," she repeated, and the words did not judge. "Then you will keep it."

He laughed once, quietly.

"I don't know how to keep anything except turning up."

"That is how." Sister Helena's answer was soft iron.

They watched candlelight play along the monstrance without fireworks. The rays pointed as they always did. They pointed outward, toward nothing the eye could measure and everything the heart stood on without naming.

"I have to send a report," Sister Helena said after a while, practical arriving as it always does after prayer. "To Rome."

Father Michael grimaced. "Will they believe it?"

"They will believe what fits their categories," she said, and the fact sounded neither bitter nor resigned. "I will tell the truth anyway."

He thought of Bishop Leonard Shaw, careful and kind, a man who had learned how to hold scandal and sacrament in the same folder without dropping either.

"He'll stand between," Father Michael said. "He always has."

Sister Helena clasped the beads once, as if closing a book.

"And you?"

He looked up at the crucifix and did not flinch.

"I'm going to say Mass," he said. "And then I'm going to sleep for ten hours, and then I'm going to visit a family who survived a miracle and see if their sink leaks, because I told Sean I'd fix it weeks ago."

She smiled with a sudden, unguarded warmth that surprised them both.

"Good. Keep promises about sinks. Demons hate the domestic."

They rose together. She touched his arm once in farewell, not habit, not ritual, just human, and then moved down the aisle to the sacristy, where forms waited to be filled and linen folded as if nothing cosmic had taken place twelve hours ago. The church survives on folded linen.

The Report

The report took longer than Sister Helena imagined it would. She wrote as she had been taught: dates, times, witnesses, phenomena observed, sacramentals used. The words looked like a case file if you didn't know how to read what lived between lines. She detailed the manifestations, levitation, xenoglossia, preternatural strength, with the deliberate coolness that allows the unbelievable to pass in rooms that distrust heat.

She did not omit the failures. A first attempt that
faltered; a priest's knees; her own memory turned against
her. She wrote names of saints invoked, litany phrases,
the point at which the demon began to echo prayer with
such precision that echo became weapon. She included
the moment when they departed the rubrics. She wrote
the line verbatim: Non in lumine, sed in fide, te conjuro
exi. She wrote that faith, not formula, drove the
sentence.

She hesitated at the Folium Obscurum section.
How does one describe a book that writes itself? She
wrote what she could without making herself a liar: the
fragment's past, the condemnations, the marginal
prophecy. She did not call it living ink. She wrote,
simply, "the letters appeared to shift under candlelight,"
which was true and not the whole truth.

She printed the pages. She signed in a hand that did
not shake. She sealed copies with wax as old as her
vows. She sent a scan through channels that had
survived inquisitions and wars and the internet, a skein
of permissions and passwords whose acronyms would
make no sense to anyone outside the Curia. She placed
the physical packet in a diplomatic pouch and entrusted
it to a monsignor who knew how not to see what he had
never been told to see.

There is a peculiar peace in doing a thing the way
you're supposed to after doing a thing no one expects

you to survive. She felt that peace now. She carried the
last copy to the altar. She placed it beneath the corporal,
a childish gesture she allowed herself.

"Let it be read rightly," she said, and "let it not be
used wrongly," and then she left the paper to paper.

The Kearns's

On campus, the bell in Gasson Hall tolled the hour
with a self-important eloquence no one begrudged it.
Elias walked beside Daniel past students dragging
backpacks, a lacrosse team in sweats, a girl crying into a
phone near Stokes like every girl has cried near Stokes
since the building acquired a door. The sky was that
enamel Boston blue you suspect is brittle.

Elias had tucked the Folium fragment into a safe he
had sworn off opening. He had printed the translation
he trusted, folded it carefully, and left it inside a book of
Augustine that still smelled faintly of a used bookstore in
Seville. He had not told Daniel where. He was learning
the difference between transparency and a new
temptation.

"I hated you," Daniel said without preface, because
sons who are priests sometimes choose the clean cut
over infection. "In college. I loved you and I hated you,
and the hatred was easier to lift."

"I deserved half of it," Elias replied, surprised by how light the sentence felt. "The other half belonged to your fear that you would become me."

Daniel laughed, and the sound had the same timbre as his chanting when he let his voice warm. "That fear kept me in the chapel longer than sincerity did."

"You stayed," Elias said.

"I stayed." Daniel's gaze slid to him. "And you... stayed last night."

"I didn't know I could," Elias admitted. The confession did not humiliate him the way it would have a year ago. Age and demons pare men down to truth whether they like it or not. "I didn't argue the shadow to death. I said amen at the right times. It felt like... not losing."

Daniel stopped near the statue of St. Ignatius raising his hand like a professor refusing an obvious answer.

"Come to Mass," he said. "Sit in the back like a lapsed academic. You can count the grammar errors in my homily."

"I'll bring a red pen," Elias said, and startled himself by grinning.

They kept walking. The wind lifted and fell. Leaves answered in their language. The boy who had once wanted to win arguments and the boy who had once wanted to be the argument himself moved in a morning that did not need them to narrate it.

Repairs

By afternoon, the glaziers had arrived at the
cathedral, their laddered truck like a secular relic on the
curb. Two men in harnesses spoke softly to the broken
rose window as if a stained-glass pope needed coaxing.
One whistled without realizing it; the melody made the
hired guard at the side door relax a notch.

In the nave, a woman named Flavia, third-
generation Polish candle lady, though no one called her
that in front of her, scraped wax with a patience you
only see in surgeons and women who keep churches
alive. She hummed a Marian hymn under her breath that
didn't match any known melody because it had been her
grandmother's, and grandmothers prefer melody to
permission.

Father Michael changed the vigil lamps before the
Blessed Sacrament. He did not hurry. He trimmed wicks
the way a man mows a lawn after a funeral, precise,
grateful for the smallness of the task. Sister Helena met
him halfway down the aisle with a roll of duct tape she
had confiscated from Daniel.

"The sacristy broom needs a splint," she said, and
he raised an eyebrow. "Even demons cannot survive
duct tape," she added, deadpan, then they both laughed

because laughing in a church when no one is looking can be one of the purest prayers.

Nora and Sean entered midafternoon with Tupperware and cautious steps, as if the building might still hold its breath. Ashlyn stayed home asleep, her nap bench-pressed into hours. They lit a candle at a side altar and stood hand in hand. Sean placed the baseball bat at the foot of St. Joseph, frowned, reconsidered, and slid it back under the pew. Joseph did not need a bat. He had a lily.

"Thank you," Nora whispered to the saint and to the people in the building and to the God she would fight with for the rest of her life and love anyway.

The city outside cared about its own liturgies: shift change, school pickup, the sudden crash at the Dunkin' two blocks over. The church inside cared about hers: psalms, dust, the ache of knees, small tools put away neatly.

Rome

Rome in late afternoon wears gold like a shrug. A sparrow chattered in the plane tree beyond the window as if the business of the Curia were only a rumor. A single candle burned on a side table, a concession to the old romance of the place. The electric lamp had an officious hum, but the candle stood its ground with a steady flame.

Cardinal Mauro Vivaldi. not the composer's descendant, though the whispers insisted on ancestry, removed his glasses and set them on the folder stamped ARCHIVUM SECRETA: 114-D. He rubbed his eyes with the heels of his hands in that exacting way men do who have taught themselves not to rub anything vulnerable.

He began at the top. He always began at the top. Report of Exorcism, Cathedral of the Holy Cross, Boston. He skimmed the first page the way old bishops skim: for nouns and dates more than adjectives. Names: Donnelly, Duarte, Kearns père et fils, Shaw. Time: night to dawn. Place: altar, nave, confessionals. Manifestations: the old list wearing a new scent. He turned the page.

The paragraph about the litany and its mirror made his mouth thin. Echo. He underlined it with a pencil he had not asked his secretary to sharpen because the wood smell comforted him. He circled non repetere verba and tapped the graphite lightly on the margin. He read the line Sister Helena had transcribed twice, then a third time, lips barely moving: Non in lumine, sed in fide, te conjuro exi. Not in light, but in faith, I conjure you to him.

He leaned back. The chair sighed in Roman. He looked up at a painting that had hung too long in this

room, a martyr with eyes rolled heavenward in a way no
living man ever rolled his eyes. Vivaldi had served under
three popes, outlasted seven scandals, buried friends and
enemies and told the truth when it could be heard. He
did not fool easily. He did not frighten easily. He read
the next page.

The Folium Obscurum section made him set down
the pencil. Not because of shock, he had read stranger,
but because his hand wanted stillness. He turned to the
appendix. Photocopies of fragments, dark as dried
pomegranate on poor paper. Marginalia impossible to
authenticate in a scan and all the more annoying for it.
He looked at the line footnoted Fragmentum 311. He
did not read it out loud. The candle flickered a fraction.
No draft. He glanced toward the window anyway.

He pressed the intercom. "Sorella?"

His secretary, a woman in her sixties who brooked
less nonsense than soldiers, entered without haste.

"Eminenza."

"Please advise the Archivum that file 114-D
remains sealed. Code riservatissimo." He tapped the
folder. "Sign and countersign. No digital duplication
beyond what has arrived. Remove the Boston name
from the index under Obscura. Cross-file it under
Adumbrationes."

"Very good." She did not ask why. She rarely did.
She had worked through the decade when why had been

a luxury the Church could not afford to answer honestly aloud.

"And... send a note to Monsignor Casati in New York," he added. "No, better: call him. There's a matter he must hear from me, not from paper, and a call to Bishop Leonard Shaw, Boston. Tonight."

She nodded. "The hour?"

"Now." The sparrow hopped on the sill, head cocked. Vivaldi watched it for an unnecessary beat and then returned to the report. He wrote in the margin in neat hand: doctrina fidei, non-formula, periculum duplicis. The danger of the double: faith and formula, the one that saves, the one that feeds the shadow if wielded badly.

When she had gone, he opened a drawer, withdrew a smaller, older folder with a binding crackled by too many hands. The first page bore a seal that tasted of smoke if you placed it to your tongue. Vienne, 1312. He laid it beside the Boston report. Across seven centuries, the same sentence ran in a thinner Latin: cum ipsa Ecclesia nomen eius invocat. He closed both files gently, as if noise could wake something.

The candle leaned, then steadied. He cupped the flame once, a superstition. Fire can be blessed and treacherous in the same minute. He let it burn.

A Kitchen Table

Back in Boston, Ashlyn woke around sunset to the smell of potatoes. Nora had cut them small and fried them too long, the way she did when her hands needed to keep busy. The sizzle held the room together. Sean hummed the wrong tune under his breath on purpose because that was how they would do it now, nothing a demon could echo perfectly.

Ashlyn sat at the kitchen table with a blanket around her shoulders and watched her parents move in their own dance. The table bore a small scorch mark from a night years ago when Patrick had learned not to set a hot pan on wood; Nora had refused to sand it out. "We live here," she had said, and tonight the sentence made the girl's throat tighten.

Father Michael sat at the corner, sleeves rolled, a red line in his palm covered with a Band-Aid patterned with cartoon sharks because the first box he found under the sink had been bought for someone else's childhood. "Cheerful," he said when he saw Nora noticing, and she laughed like a woman surprised by her own mouth.

Sister Helena arrived with bread she had pretended to buy and actually baked in a convent kitchen that still knows how to warm a house. Elias brought a bottle of something expensive he had been saving for a different kind of celebration. Daniel set plates.

They ate too much and not enough. No one dared name the miracle. They spoke instead of garlic and traffic and whether the Sox might finally make a clean series out of the mess they kept choosing. Sean told a story about Patrick that had grown more lovable in the telling; Ashlyn laughed and the sound made time do a small, private bow.

When the plates were cleared and the night had decided against rain, Sister Helena rose. "I leave tomorrow," she said, and the table received the words without dropping forks. "Rome wants paper."

"You'll come back?" Ashlyn asked. Her voice did not shake, and the steadiness felt like someone else's gift.

"If I'm sent," Sister Helena said, then amended of her own will, "and if you need me." She placed a hand lightly on the girl's head. "But I think you won't."

Ashlyn lifted her own hand and laid it over Sister Helena's. "Still," she said, and there was room in the single word for gratitude and a child's reasonable selfishness.

"I'll write," Elias offered, smiling ruefully at himself. "Not about this. About whatever you like. Fish. Poetry. History when it isn't trying to eat us."

"Fish," Ashlyn said, surprising them, and the table laughed in that relieved way people do when men say fish and mean an angel.

Father Michael stood. "I should get back," he said. "There's a vigil." He meant a nap.

Sean stopped him at the doorway and folded him into a hug that lifted the priest an inch off his feet; Father Michael's laugh came out strangled and joyful. "Thank you," Sean said in his ear, and on the old reflex to deflect, Father Michael nearly said, don't, but instead answered, "You're welcome," because receiving gratitude is its own obedience.

In the street, the night lay gentle. He stepped off the stoop into air that smelled like city water and fried onions and the kind of quiet that follows a long day.

His phone vibrated.

The Call

"Father Donnelly? Leonard Shaw." The bishop's voice kept its careful calm, but underneath it, Father Michael heard the thread they both recognized now: a man trying to give worry only the exact space it warrants.

"Bishop. I was just thinking of you." He had been, about paperwork and pastoral care and the way Leonard had stood invisible in the shadows of the nave, using authority like scaffolding and not like a blade.

"Good," Shaw said. "I apologize for the hour." Father Michael glanced at his watch. It was not late enough to deserve apology; bishops apologize anyway when Rome calls after Vespers.

"What's happened?"

"A call from Rome." A pause, the kind that can curdle or bless. "From Cardinal Vivaldi. He wanted me to hear it from him, not by cable. There's... a development."

Father Michael stopped under a streetlight. A moth traced spastic geometry in the glow. "Tell me."

"Do you remember the relic found in Mosul? The one in your report, the fragment that traveled to Boston the long way, through loss."

Father Michael's palm ached as if the skin remembered more than mind. "I remember."

"They believe there was a second object taken during the raids," Shaw said. His voice stayed measured; his breath did not. "Not catalogued. Not declared. Sold off the books."

"To whom?" Father Michael asked, though in his bones he dreaded the answer's shape more than its letters.

"Not to whom. To where." Shaw exhaled. "New York."

Father Michael shut his eyes. He saw bridges, subways, a fat old city that chews and prays and spits and sings. He pictured a relic in the wrong hands in a borough that could hide anything behind a deli counter and a locked back room. "What is it?"

"They're not sure. A reliquary, perhaps. A vessel. The description is... inconsistent." Paper rustled, the bishop finding the place with his finger. "An 'ark,' one source says, but we suspect metaphor. A chest, more likely, with an inner lining of... vellum."

"Written?" Father Michael asked, throat dry.

"Possibly." Shaw's voice dipped. "The dealer who brokered it disappeared last month. The buyer's name is redacted. Vivaldi thinks the trail runs through a private collection attached to a foundation on the Upper East Side. He asked whether we had anyone who could move quietly."

Father Michael said nothing for a heartbeat that counted for a decision. The streetlight hummed. A car door slammed two blocks away. In the Sullivan kitchen, laughter rose and fell like tide. In Rome, a candle refused to die.

"Sister Helena leaves in the morning," Father Michael said. "Kearns could track a whisper in a cyclone. Daniel speaks Upper East Side in his old tuxedo and sneakers. I can carry a crucifix where it needs to be and keep my mouth closed when curiosity is a sin."

Shaw's relief arrived not as breath but as silence relaxing. "I'll ask for the file. We keep this small, Father Michael. Quiet. Not because I'm afraid of scandal." A dry, almost amused note colored the word. "Because he feeds on echo. We starve him of it."

Father Michael looked down at his palm, at the shark sticker barely holding down the wound. "Understood."

Shaw hesitated, then added, rare softness rounding his Boston vowels: "You don't have to do this."

"I know," Father Michael said simply. He did. "But I think we're already doing it."

"Very well." Shaw's tone settled into the weight of a plan. "I'll call you at eight. Pack for one night. We'll pretend it is that."

"Bishop?"

"Yes."

"Thank you," Father Michael said. The line hummed with all the meanings men force into the sentence when they are careful with praise. "For... not naming it too soon. For standing back and standing with."

"Go sleep, Father," Shaw replied, and Father Michael heard something like affection, a thing the bishop disguised under diocesan calm because love and bureaucracy share poor plumbing. "Tomorrow will be longer than it deserves."

They clicked off. Father Michael stood in the pool of light and let his eyes adjust to dark. A whistle blew somewhere, a train perhaps, or a boy pretending. He put the phone in his pocket beside the blue glass slice. It nipped his knuckles as if to say wake up.

He turned back to the Sullivan's door. Through the curtain he saw the silhouette of a girl at a table, her head tilted toward her mother's laughter, the tilt that means a body has decided to stay.

He put his hand on the doorknob and did not turn it. Some moments you do not enter; you guard them from the porch.

He looked down Tremont toward the cathedral and then east toward a city that glitters and hides and sells even its mysteries in daylight. He squared his shoulders in the way his mother had scolded him for, "you'll ruin your jacket", and smiled at the memory because jackets can be mended and sometimes you choose the ruin that fits your back.

In Rome, the candle steadied. The cardinal closed a file and opened his phone.

In Boston, a bishop scrolled to a number labeled Casati and pressed call.

In New York, a locked door in a private gallery made a noise no human ear would have admitted to hearing.

And on O'Reilly Street, a priest stood in the ordinary dark, felt the weight of a crucifix and a shard of blue glass in his pocket, and understood that the shadow had not ended so much as retreated to where shadows go, into the corners where men think light is optional.

"Not in light," he said under his breath to no one listening and the One who always did, "but in faith."

He turned away from the door and walked into the night, where the city was already setting its stage for whatever comes when a story refuses to be finished.